FAIRY TALES
FROM THE ROCK
A COLLECTION OF SHORT STORIES

Library and Archives Canada Cataloguing in Publication information is available upon request.

ISBN-13: 978-1-77478-126-5

Copyright © 2023 Engen Books

Introduction © 2023 Erin Vance
Fair Warning © 2023 Ash Greening
The Swan © 2023 Bronwynn Erskine
Grouchy and the Old, Mean Moose © 2023 Melissa Wong
Mine Own © 2023 Sharon Selby
The Riddle-Game © 2023 Isobel Granby
Wolves in the Woods © 2023 Stacey Oakley
The Sleeping Giant of Conception Bay South © 2023 Melissa Bishop
Bedtime Stories © 2023 Ryan Belbin
The Beat of a Different Drone © 2023 Corinne Lewandowski
Snow White and the Seven D.W.A.R.F.S © 2023 Heather Reilly
Scarlett Hood © 2023 Teresita E. Dziadura
The Three Sisters © 2023 Lisa M Daly
Pinochio's Puppet © 2023 Eve Morton
Rumperella © 2023 Lena Ng
Poultice © 2023 David James Lynch
Captured Land © 2023 W.H.Vigo
Every Child a Changeling © 2023 Ainsley Hawthorn

NO PART OF THIS BOOK MAY BE REPRODUCED OR TRANSMITTED IN ANY FORM OR BY ANY MEANS, ELECTRONIC OR MECHANICAL, INCLUDING PHOTOCOPYING AND RECORDING, OR BY ANY INFORMATION STORAGE OR RETRIEVAL SYSTEM WITHOUT WRITTEN PERMISSION FROM THE COPYRIGHT HOLDER, EXCEPT FOR BRIEF PASSAGES QUOTED IN A REVIEW.

This book is a work of fiction. Names, characters, places and incidents are products of each author's imagination or are used fictitiously. Any resemblance to actual events or locales or persons living or dead is entirely coincidental.

Distributed by:
Engen Books
www.engenbooks.com
submissions@engenbooks.com
First mass market paperback printing: May 2023
Cover Image: © 2022 Graham Blair Designs

FAIRY TALES
FROM THE ROCK
EDITED BY ERIN VANCE AND ELLEN CURTIS

ENGEN
BOOKS

Introduction
Erin Vance

Once upon a time, fairy tales were all we had.

They were tales to explain the unexplained, to impart morality and culture, to share histories and truths; but more than not, to warn.

Fairy tales are so entangled with our concept of what makes us human that it is, perhaps, odd that so many stories are about the other: the fae, the monsters in the forest, princesses, and heroes. Magic and transformations are not unusual in fairy tales, although they are often terrible — not necessarily evil, but certainly awful. Wishes can come true in stories, although there may be a price to pay, and bravery and a kind heart are rewarded with happily-ever-afters. These are concepts that we still teach our children and even try to live by as adults. There is a simple kind of morality in these stories, despite the grey that exists in both worlds.

When choosing stories for this anthology, we tried to find readaptations or retellings, modernizations or even twists on the original fairy tales — even a handful of original fairy tales. Despite this, we wanted to keep to the heart of what fairy tales have always been, not only for nostalgia's sake, but because the truths of fairy tales are still the truths of today. We wish to celebrate goodness, courage in the face of evil, embracing one's true self, and choosing to be kind.

In this collection, we have a wide range of stories we are very excited to share with you. Stories about princesses who find their worth in how they can serve as opposed to be served, about accepting who you truly are and letting it change you (often literally, since these stories have a touch of magic), and about consciences that aren't just a voice in your head or heart, but maybe an animal guide coaxing you down a path. Maybe true love isn't a person, but freedom, maybe your history is your future, and those that are lost can still be found.

We are so pleased to lead you through truly excellent stories and hope they bring you as much warmth and enjoyment as they did to us. Enjoy rescues and hero's quests and an abundance of kindness.

Erin Vance
Editor

CONTENTS

Erin Vance
Introduction..005

Ash Greening
Fair Warning..009

Bronwynn Erskine
The Swan..012

Melissa Wong
Grouchy and the Old, Mean Moose................................029

Sharon Selby
Mine Own..034

Isobel Granby
The Riddle-Game...046

Stacey Oakley
Wolves in the Woods..061

Melissa Bishop
The Sleeping Giant of Conception Bay South.................073

Ryan Belbin
Bedtime Stories..087

Corinne Lewandowski
The Beat of a Different Drone..............................099

Heather Reilly
Snow White and the Seven D.W.A.R.F.S.........................131

Teresita E. Dziadura
Scarlett Hood..140

Lisa M Daly
The Three Sisters...170

Eve Morton
Pinochio's Puppet..193

Lena Ng
Rumperella..206

David James Lynch
Poultice..216

W.H.Vigo
Captured Land...244

Ainsley Hawthorn
Every Child a Changeling 261

Graham Blair Designs
On the Cover...271

Fair Warning

Leave the world behind you and cross into the Green.
Come to see the Faerie Courts and watch the Dance Unseen.
Listen to the bargains stuck by word and blood and bone.
Come present your offering to the Regent on her throne.

Is it wealth you seek, my dear, your coins of petty gold?
Bits of metal that mean naught against winter's biting cold.
Or is it love you're chasing along the springtime breeze?
Swayed with little effort, for hearts are bent with ease.

Perhaps it's vines of hatred that burn like summer's sun.
We'll grant your vengeance, darling, but you'll pay us when it's done.
Or is it autumn's death that's come knocking at your door?
Are you sure it's worth the price to live a season more?

Come and share our bounty for an hour or a day;
Don't forget that what we give, we can also take away.
Accept only what you're offered, ask for nothing more,
Or when you go to leave, alas, you will not find the door.

Always read the fine print in the writing on the wall;
And have your payment ready when we come to call.
Ask your favours, mortals, but do not slight the Queen,
Lest you wish to wander always, lost among the Green.

Ash Greening

Ash Greening is an author from Eastern Newfoundland. Their fiction has appeared previously in *Kit Sora: The Artobiography* (Engen Books), *Whisper Sweet Nothings* (WANL), *Folklore Next Door* (WANL), and *Sea Stories from the Rock*.

Their first novel, *Sea Change*, is expected in late 2023 or early 2024 from Engen Books.

They brought with them the preceding poem, *Fair Warning*, arranged first for flow.

Bronwynn Erskine

Bronwynn Erskine is an Ontario native currently residing in Newfoundland. Erskine is an avid steampunk enthusiast and acrylic landscape painter.

Erskine made their publishing debut in 2018's *Chillers from the Rock* with their chilling tale: "Scarlett Ribbons," returned in 2019's *Flights from the Rock* with "Feather and Bone," with "The Lindwyrm's Bride" in *Mythology from the Rock*, and was featured with three stories in *Acceptance: Stories at the Centre of Us*.

In May 2023 they released their first novel, *By Reservation Only*.

The Swan

The sun rises on another beautiful day at the palace, and I wake from a restless slumber. Once I would not have dreamed of being up so early. But that was before. Now I'm grateful to escape the dreams that haunt me almost every night, and in any case, I have much to do.

Yesterday I taunted the hounds in their kennels to such a fervor that they snapped at the Duke of Carlisle when he attempted to gather the pack and take the Queen on a hunting excursion. His high-pitched squawk was quite satisfying. The hounds bayed all afternoon, and I heard one of the Queen's ladies saying that Her Majesty had taken to her bed with a headache from all the noise. The hounds are tired from all their excitement now, and in any case, I don't want to become too predictable. But there are plenty of other things for me to do.

I paddle out from among the reeds that surround the marshy islet where I've made my nest. I always loved the lake on the palace grounds. Sometimes, I try to put a brighter face on my situation by reminding myself of all the times my governesses denied me the opportunity to swim here. It helps a little, some days. Mostly I try to keep busy, to keep my mind on other things.

I stretch my wings up towards the paling blue of the sky and feel the wind caress my silky white feathers. There's pleasure in this, even if it's not a pleasure I'm long familiar with. My wings are strong and my neck is graceful, and I am lovely now where once I was rather plain. And no one dares tell me what I may not do.

Taking flight is a bit ungainly, a lot of flapping that still feels undignified, but once I'm in the air I feel at home. I love flying even more than I love swimming. I gain enough height to survey the grounds and circle slowly, watching the palace and its occupants wake for another day. Movement in the kitchen garden catches my eye. I would smirk if I still had a mouth that could perform such an action. Yes, that will do very nicely to start my day. I angle my wings and glide downward.

The cook's assistant pauses just outside the door to yawn and adjust his hose. When he opens his eyes again, I am standing in the middle of the herb garden. Some of the more fragile plants have already been crushed by my careless wings, and others will be trampled beneath my webbed feet in the altercation to come. His eyes widen, and I glare back with beady black eyes and all the malice a swan can muster. Swans are very good at malice, I've learned, in spite of their graceful appearance.

He takes a cautious step, angling sideways. The fresh spinach leaves, plump tomatoes, and tender sprigs of basil that he came out here to gather for the Queen's breakfast table are still intact, for now. I never knew they did that every morning, before. It's amazing the things I didn't know, in spite of living my entire life within these palace walls. He might think he can gather them and get out of here, and let me be someone else's problem later in the day when they need carrots to be glazed for supper and the rosemary I'm standing in to season the venison roast. If that's what he thinks, he's going to be disappointed. He takes another step, and I narrow my eyes.

I spread my wings a bit, stretch out my long, long neck in his direction, and hiss.

He flinches and stumbles back with clumsy steps, treading carelessly on a squash vine that's escaped the edge of its plot. Oh yes, he knows the malice a swan is capable of.

I honk and stomp aggressively forward, wings fanning wide now. They batter against the herbs, breaking stems and crushing delicate blossoms.

With a startled squeak, he drops his kitchen shears and bolts. Back to the door and the safety of the kitchen.

Through the open door, I can hear raised voices. The cook isn't a particularly soft-spoken man, nor is he known among the staff for a sweet temper. There's a part of me that feels guilty for getting the assistant in trouble. It's only a small part though. There's only so many things a swan is capable of, and most of them can't touch the Queen directly.

Listening with one ear to the argument inside, I waddle in the direction the assistant cook was heading. Spinach and tomatoes with her breakfast are an important part of the Queen's routine, and they're well within the reach of a swan. I eat the spinach carelessly, ripping plants up by their roots and scattering them across the garden bed and the path. The tomatoes have an unsettling texture when my beak bites into them, but I can still rip them from their vines and stomp them into the dirt in order to deny them to her.

The voices from inside fall silent around the time I'm starting on the herbs. I hear footsteps. I look up, imperious with an entire thyme plant dangling from my beak, to see the cook's assistant has returned. He's not alone this time. I think the other two are kitchen boys. None of them look pleased to be here, but I'm certainly pleased to see them. My small, webbed feet can only do so much damage, but they've all got big, sturdy shoes perfect for trampling gardens.

I honk in challenge, letting the thyme fall, and rip off a beakful of savoury.

The gardens are laid out so that every part of them can be reached from the narrow paths between, but it's hard for them to place their feet carefully when they're running to try and catch me, or flailing backwards to try and avoid being bitten. Swans have a powerful bite when they choose to use it. The fair-haired kitchen boy howls as he learns this firsthand, and topples over backwards, flailing, into a bed of nearly ripe zucchini. Vines break beneath him and tangle around his limbs.

Evidently getting tired of the farce, the cook himself steps outside to take the situation in hand. He's just in time to see his assistant trample through the strawberries, bent double as he tries to grab me. I quickly duck under the lowest rung of the trellis that supports the bean plants, but he can't stop in time and crashes straight into it. The cook shouts something in a language I don't know. I'm not sure if it's aimed at me or the assistant, but I turn my head and honk anyway.

That's when I see the big carving knife he's got in one meaty hand. No one is supposed to harm the swans on the palace grounds, but maybe he doesn't remember that. Maybe he's angry enough that he doesn't care right now.

Or maybe the Queen revoked her late husband's edict protecting them. That's a possibility I hadn't thought of before, and it chills me more than the coldest winter night spent huddled down in my nest on the islet. The late King loved the swans more than anything except his daughter, but the Queen was never fond of them. And swan is considered good eating in many places. Maybe the cook is hoping a nice plump swan for the supper table will make up for the missing spinach and tomatoes, and whatever else we've managed to destroy.

I mantle my wings and give him my most defiant hiss, but all the joy has gone out of it now. I push myself back into the sky in search of something else that needs my attention. There must be something.

It's late and growing dark by the time I return to the lake. I chased the gardeners for much of the day. They had more self-preservation instincts than the kitchen staff, and I managed to get fairly free rein over their vaunted roses and rhododendrons. I made a point of eating the peony blossoms, which I know the Queen enjoys having in her dressing room, and of shitting on the rim of her favourite fountain.

I want to call it a day well spent, but I don't know. The cook's knife still has me rattled.

I paddle around the lake for a bit. I'm not hungry for water weeds, not after all the other things I ate while terrorising the gardens, but I dabble a bit just for the sensation of it. Sometimes, ducking my head under the water and reaching for the soft green depths is a comfort. Sometimes it lets me shut out the world and just be for a few moments. It doesn't much help today.

When the sun is little more than a thin rim of gold on the horizon, I give in and swim to the decorative island in the middle of the lake. It's a prettier, but less isolated spot than my own tiny islet. This one has carved stone benches like it was once meant for small, intimate moments away from the noise of garden parties, but it's been abandoned to the swans for many years now. They nest there and raise their downy cygnets beneath the bowers once so carefully tended.

I don't venture near very often. Maybe it makes no difference, maybe the denizens of the palace can't tell one swan from another, but I don't like to chance it. I don't want any of the others to be blamed for my actions. But tonight, I can't quite bear to retire to my solitary nest.

I climb out of the water, shake a few stray droplets from my feathers, and waddle up the slope. The wild swans watch me. They know I'm different from them, even if they can't comprehend what the difference is, but they're not exactly unfriendly. Just a little standoffish. I can hardly blame them for that, wild things that they are. They nest in twos and sometimes threes, each nest with its own defined space. The island is safer than the shore, even on a lake where no one has been allowed to hunt them for decades, and so they put up with each others' proximity in order to have a spot here.

On the highest point of the island, at the crest of a decorative embankment where the feral rosebushes don't offer enough cover to break the autumn winds when they come wailing down out of the mountains, there's a spot not claimed by any nest. It's still summer now, and this exposed spot is no great hardship. I nestle down into the tangled grasses and preen my feathers free of any lingering water.

The wild swans settle again when they see I'm only here to do swan things amongst them. They watch my campaign against the Queen and her court without understanding, but I'm pretty sure they do watch. I see them sometimes on the banks of the lake, peering up towards the palace and whatever ruckus I'm causing that day.

They aren't my friends, but then I never had many of those to begin with. Not real friends who cared about me for my own sake. The wild swans, at least, make no pretense to fond feelings for me just to curry favour from my father. They tolerate me here on their island on the nights when my despair grows too overwhelming to face alone. It's all the friendship they have to offer, perhaps. I am more grateful for it than I have the words to tell.

Surrounded by the quiet presence of the wild swans, I sleep for once without dreams. It's still early when I wake. I don't move, my head still tucked under one wing, and listen to the world around me. If it wasn't my nightmares that woke me, it was something else. I want to know what before I make any move that might betray my location, especially with the other swans dozing all around me.

Something splashes in the water. A high, feminine voice squeals with laughter. Several others shush and giggle.

If I had eyebrows, they would surely be rising. No one should be down by the lake at this hour, but someone clearly is. Whatever is a swan to do about that?

I unfold myself, not raising my head too high so I'll remain hidden in the overgrown brush, and waddle down to the water on the far side of the island. I swim away first before circling back.

It's not hard to spot them. Three beautiful maidens, all with the thick black hair and sun-kissed skin of the southern kingdoms, are playing in the shallows by an overhanging willow tree. They giggle and splash each other, the water sparking rainbows from the early morning sun and making their long hair gleam as slick and sleek as ravens' feathers.

They must be guests at court because I would surely remember if I'd seen them before. Perhaps no one thought to warn them of the lake's dangers. Or perhaps they went in spite of the warning. Either way their pretty white gowns lie discarded on the bank, as tempting a target as I've ever seen.

I climb up onto the bank some distance from them and sidle over. It's almost too easy. I snatch one dress and waddle swiftly off into the underbrush with it, and they don't even look up from their games. The second joins it. It's only when I come back for the third dress that one of them catches sight of me. She points me out to her friends, and they exclaim, shushing each other again to avoid frightening me off. How charming that they think I might be so shy.

I walk closer, right up to the patch of grass where the third woman's dress lies neatly folded. I meet their eyes, staring straight at them, bold and lovely as ever a swan has been. Then, in a single graceful movement, I dip my neck down, snatch up the dress, and whirl away.

Their cries of dismay follow me as I sprint across the grass, rising even higher when they leave the water and see the other two dresses are missing as well. They pull on their shifts (I may have malice in my lovely heart, but I am not so cruel as to leave them without any garments), and chase after me.

Swans can run surprisingly fast for short stretches, but we aren't made for distance running. I have to dodge and weave to stay ahead of them. I could fly away, or even swim, but I find I don't want to. There's a pleasure to this chase that's every bit as fierce as I felt chasing the gardeners.

I didn't set out to join their games, but I realise belatedly that I have. The women laugh as they chase me. Their cheeks are flushed and their shifts cling to their damp skin, and they laugh as they try to trap me and trick me. If I could, I would laugh with them. I let them think they've got me, then dive between them at the last moment, and their reaching fingers brush the softness of my feathers as I pass. I would play this game forever, if I could.

Even as I think that, it all comes crashing down. One of the women gives a startled cry and they all fall silent. When I look back, I see a young lord from the Queen's court has ridden up from the direction of the woods at the end of the lake, coming upon the scene with all of us unaware.

He looks over the women, all dressed in naught but their shifts, and I do not like the look of the smile that curls his lips. I think they must not either. They cluster together, clinging to each other, trying to draw themselves and each other away from his hungry gaze.

He swings down from the saddle with careless grace, still looking. His gaze would be unseemly even if they were fully clothed, and his smirk suggest he knows this. And more, he knows there's nothing they can do about it.

They're refined and noble ladies. They might allow themselves an occasional hint of mischief like sneaking out to play in the lake when no one will see, but they're far too well-bred and well-mannered to have a hope of defending themselves against a man like him. I can see it all as clear as if it were laid out in front of me, how this will go.

I do not have lips, but even so I can almost feel them curl in disdain. All my life I was taught to sit quietly, eyes demurely lowered, while men like him looked their fill.

But I am not a princess any longer. I have spent the months of my exile exploring and embracing the malice of a swan's heart, and I no longer care to be told what I may or must not do.

I lay the dress aside on the grass and return to where the maidens cower before the bold young lordling. Lowering my head and stretching out my long, long neck, I hiss with all the fury that burned within me under my stepmother's stifling hand.

He startles at the sound.

The maidens do as well. They had heard my honk while I teased them, but not my hiss. The hiss of an angry swan had seemed too harsh when all I intended to offer them was alarm and inconvenience.

The lord recovers quickly, but his smirk has grown slightly hollow. I remember, vaguely, that he is one of Duke Carlisle's hunting companions, though I still can't recall his name. He knows enough of swans to be wary of me.

His gaze flicks past me to the maidens, and his expression firms. Not wary enough, it seems, to pass up what he thinks is a golden opportunity. The smirk turns cruel. Crueler, anyway. He draws a hunting knife that's sheathed at his belt and takes a step towards me, teeth bared.

"Here, pretty birdy," he croons, eyes sparkling with anticipation.

In the face of that hungry expression, I wonder suddenly about Carlisle and his rumoured relationship with the Queen. Whether it's truly what I thought it was. Whether she is.

But there's no time for that line of questioning right now. He takes another step, clearly expecting me to back off. He might know a little of swans, but not enough. Even a wild swan would hold her ground if she was already angry enough to posture the way I have been.

Instead, I rush him, wings flapping and honking my most aggressive honks. He knows to avoid a strike from my beak but forgets that my wings are the real danger. Swans are large and it takes a lot of muscle to carry us aloft. I bring all that muscle to bear now, slapping furiously at him with widely spread wings. The impacts jar through me, but from his startled yells I think they must be worse to him.

He scrambles back, stumbles, and falls to the ground. I can't stop now. The maidens are still cowering like frightened cygnets behind me, too shocked and frightened to seize the opportunity I've created for them and run. I don't entirely mind. Continuing to buffet the lord with my powerful wings is no hardship. Until it is.

I forgot to keep track of the knife. That was careless of me, I know. But even yesterday, when the cook's cleaver shocked me so, I suppose I had not truly lost my trust in the edict against harming the swans.

Now the pain is a bright, sharp thing with a life of its own inside my breast.

My hiss is as much a gasp. A breathy sound, defiant but without much strength remaining.

His grin is triumphant in spite of the rising bruises. I bite his face. He shrieks and flings me back with more strength than I expect, so I bounce on the trampled turf. The pain jars through me, rattles my breath and my bones.

I manage to raise my head, just a little, and give him my best remaining glare.

He's breathing hard, clothing smeared with dirt and blood. Several fingers bend at the wrong angle and it looks like there's something wrong with one leg. None of that compares to his face.

I've never bitten anyone before, for all the trouble I've caused. I knew I could do damage. There's something like little teeth on the inside of my beak and the edges of my tongue, and I can put a lot of force behind them. The wound is worse than I expected though. It's hard to make out through the blood, but it looks ragged.

And he's still shrieking. He tries to clutch at it, but can't seem to decide between the hand with the probably-broken fingers and the one still clutching the bloody knife.

I should do something, but I don't know what.

Then something touches my sprawled wing. I flinch, try to jerk away but the pain in my chest is too big. It's one of the maidens. She has a birthmark peeking out from the neckline of her shift, and blue, blue eyes like summer twilight. I stop struggling as she folds my uncoordinated wings in close to my body and gathers me up. There are worse places to die than the arms of a beautiful woman.

"We've got to bind up the wound," she says. I don't think she's talking to me, but it doesn't matter. I couldn't answer even if she was.

"We've got to get away," one of her companions says, clutching at her shoulder and pulling her along. "Someone will hear him, and come, and we can't be here when they do."

"Do you think he won't tell everyone what he saw?" the woman carrying me asks. Her voice is sharp and angry, but her hands are still gentle.

"I think he will have other things to worry about, at least for a time," says the third girl. She's holding the reins of a horse, a placid gray mare, not the hunter's high-strung bay. "Quickly, my lady. You cannot be found here."

The other two shepherd her into the mare's saddle, still in her shift and cradling me to her chest, then press handkerchiefs into her hands to hold against my wound.

"Ride quickly, my lady," one of the other maidens says sternly. "We will follow when we've found our gowns, so there is no trace of us here."

I manage to lift me head from the lady's shoulder and honk quietly. She tries to shush me, but I point with my beak towards the bushes where I hid the first two stolen dresses. A hint of white fabric is just visible through the leaves.

The lady laughs, but the sound breaks halfway into a sob. "You are incorrigible," she whispers, and leans down to kiss my bloody beak. "You are the most ridiculous creature."

The kiss makes me feel strange. Or maybe it's the wound in my chest. I feel lighter, light as a bit of down carried on the wind, with none of the ungainly flapping to get myself aloft.

The mare may be a placid lady's mount, but she has a good gait. She runs swift and sure, and I feel as if I'm flying again, one last time, even as I leave a trail of unravelling white feathers behind us. I don't know why my feathers are falling off. I stare up at them, lifting into the air above us, each one trimmed with sunrise gold as it dissolves. At this rate I will have no feathers left by the time we reach the guesthouse.

The lady's staff have been watching for her. A groom is waiting to take the horse's reins before she's even stopped. Another moves close to help her down but draws back with a strangled cry when he sees me.

"Hurry," she tells them. "There is no time for delicacy. Help me get her down and send for my nurse."

I don't understand what's going on. Surely they've seen a swan before. I'm not making a fuss now, so I don't know why the grooms are so ginger about handling me. Someone brings a blanket to wrap me up in. They must think I'll bite someone else. That must be it.

They hurry me inside and the lady rushes after me even as they try to fuss over her state of undress.

Another woman appears, older and darker complexioned, with skin that smells of herbs when she brushes my hair back from my face. "Bring her into the kitchen. It's closer," she orders imperiously.

"Will she be alright?" the lady asks, hovering uncertainly when her servants lay me on the big, smooth wooden counter. "She saved us."

The nurse's hands are already moving, pushing back the blanket and wiping blood from my chest. "You wouldn't have needed saving if you hadn't gone out unescorted," she replies distractedly.

"I don't want to live in a pretty golden cage," the lady says. It has the feel of an old argument, worn smooth with repetition where the two have had it many times before. She clasps my hand between hers and rubs her thumb over the bones of my wrist. "And I wouldn't have found her, if I hadn't gone out. Do you think she's the missing princess?"

There's a new flurry of activity as the other two maidens come in, and I lose the thread of the conversation going on above me. Why should the lady think a swan is the missing princess? Even if she's right.

My human body, feeling strangely heavy and ungainly after so many months, is dressed in a gown borrowed from one of Countess Basira's ladies by the time someone from the palace proper arrives. Basira is still fretting about the dress, a plain one of dove grey linen, and wishing one of her own more elaborate ones could have fit me. But I've nearly a head of height on her, if I could gather the strength to stand, and it simply isn't happening.

She sits next to me on the settee in the parlour, trying not to fuss, but I can see the wanting to in her expression. In the way she tugs her lip between her teeth, and the marks it leaves in the paint her ladies applied there. I'm staring too long, looking at her lips and thinking things I shouldn't. Things that were the reason my stepmother took the drastic measures she did in the first place. But in my defence, they're very nice lips.

I make myself look away, towards the door, so I see the palace guard when he enters. I see his carefully neutral expression crumble into shock as he recognises me.

He drops the helm tucked neatly under his arm and stands there, open mouthed.

"I do appreciate your timely arrival," I tell him, when I think he's had enough time to gape. "Please inform Her Highness of my return. I will be staying here for a time before I rejoin the court. I expect there will be no difficulty in having my affects delivered. Thank you."

Still unable to speak, the guard makes a shaky bow and departs. Halfway out the door, he obviously remembers about the helm. He turns again, grabs it off the floor, bows again, and hurries out.

Beside me, Basira giggles prettily behind a fan. Her eyes gleam wickedly above the painted silk.

Melissa Wong

Melissa Wong is a freelance multimedia creator. A MUN alumni with a B.A. (Hons) and a diploma in journalism, Wong's short story "Chirp", won the 2021 Icelandic Festival of Manitoba: Poetry and Pose contest and was published in the festival program. Wong's creative writing has been published in The Newfoundland Herald, Truth Serum Press, Pure Slush, Applebeard, the Icelandic Connection Magazine, the Understorey Magazine, WANL Winter E-Zine, and Engen Books' newsletters. Her latest poem "Burger Meditations" was published in

Cow Pure Slush Vol. 23. Born and raised in St. John's, Newfoundland, Wong spends most of her free time making YouTube videos, backyard gardening, and painting.

Grouchy and the Old, Mean Moose

Once upon a time, there lived an angry moose who tormented all the folks in a small Newfoundland town. One of these folks was a farmer named Grouchy who had a long history with the moose. In one adventure, the moose had torn open the fence to get to the farmer's crabapples and had scared the man's poor cows. Unfortunately, the townspeople were reluctant to track the majestic animal for fear they might hurt him; and so, the moose continued to be a problem.

One day, Grouchy found his cow, Duckie, crying in terror. Nothing he could do would help calm down Duckie, and he suspected the moose had tried to attack the cow. Grouchy felt a deep hurt inside his ribcage from his pure helplessness. Duckie was the one cow that would come by when Grouchy played his flute. She loved music. Grouchy picked up his flute and played for Duckie, hoping it might soothe her.

All of the animals stopped to listen to his music. One of them was a Newfoundland pine marten. The pine martin jumped out of the woods, climbed onto the damaged fence, and sat near Grouchy's left foot, waiting for the song to finish.

As soon as the last note faded away, the pine marten spoke: "You must go to the moose and tell him that he's getting old, and no one fears him anymore."

"He will only attack me," said Grouchy.

"Not if you say that the people fear you," said the pine martin. "Challenge him to walk behind you into town. People will run away from you in fear."

Before Grouchy could say another word to argue, the pine martin ran away. The farmer thought about the pine martin's advice before he went to find the moose.

However, the angry moose found the farmer first.

In the daylight, Grouchy realized the moose was quite old and seemed rather sick. Maybe that was why he flew into a rage whenever someone made too much noise. However, despite their old age, the moose prepared to attack the farmer.

Before the moose could strike him down, Grouchy called out, "You are getting old, moose, and no one fears you anymore. I took your place. Walk behind me into town, and people will run away from me."

"Very well," said the moose. "But I will tear you apart if the townspeople do not run away!"

"Very well," said Grouchy, his stomach falling with fear. However, for the sake of his farm and his town, he refused to show it.

The moose followed the farmer into town, and when the people saw the farmer with the moose behind him, they ran away. Mothers fled in terror, fathers backed away with wide eyes, and children picked up their puppies and ran for home.

When the pair reached the heart of the town, the farmer said, "I proved it. People run from me now."

The moose was trembling too much to speak because that mean old moose had not realized that the townspeople were actually running away from him

Before this walk, Grouchy had thought he would punish the moose. He thought that perhaps the beast's rage would infect him, and Grouchy believed he would explode in anger — much like the moose always had in the past.

But that didn't happen.

Grouchy had always seen the moose as a monster, but when he saw the beast vulnerable and sad, the fire of Grouchy's righteous anger faded. Instead, he only felt pity.

"You are getting old, moose," said Grouchy. "Let me take care of you. You can stay at my farm. Walk behind me to my farm, and I will show you where you can stay."

"Very well," said the scared moose.

The farmer led the moose to his farm and showed the moose a nice pen. It was warm with nice wooden boards and fresh food available for the moose to eat. The moose agreed to stay and entered the pen. Grouchy closed the gate behind the moose and so managed to capture that moose without hurting anyone.

As time passed and the moose had a full belly, a warm, peaceful place to sleep, and Grouchy's music to heal the heart, the moose realized the harm he had caused and, with Duckie's permission, that moose visited the cows and apologized for terrorizing them.

Indeed, the moose was too old to terrorize anyone anymore. Grouchy was at peace with caring for the moose, Duckie, and the other animals in their old age. He vowed to treat the moose better than that moose had treated the townspeople, and made sure other animals knew that his farm was a safe place to stay if need be.

At last, the town was at peace.

Sharon Selby

Sharon Selby is a Canadian professor of Professional Communications and English Literature at Fanshawe College in London, ON.

They bring with them their original short story "Mine Own."

In addition to "Mine Own," they have published several academic reviews and articles, as well as an academic monograph on the relationship between memory and identity in Canadian literature.

Mine Own

Dee had been sitting in the garden for over an hour, her cup of tea cold and forgotten. Leaves rustled in the autumn wind, whispering amongst themselves like secretive school children. The longer she sat, the more she felt that she could almost understand them.

They'd found the Roadside Wilds B&B off the main road. They'd gotten lost an hour or so outside of Armadale, having just left the ferry that had brought them to the Isle of Skye. Eventually, they'd had to stop as neither of them trusted the GPS or the narrow winding roads in the encroaching twilight. They'd intended merely to ask for directions, but the place itself had spoken to them — quaint, tidy, and run by an eccentric old lady who truly knew the meaning of a full Scottish breakfast. They'd passed a quiet but pleasant evening drinking the old lady's scotch, then feasted in the morning on sausage, bacon, *and* black pudding. At some point, Dee's husband had begun cross-examining their hostess about local history. The old lady, who insisted they call her "Auntie," had seen Dee's eyes glaze as Brad jotted notes on his paper napkin about yet another war memorial in a nearby village, and had offered them something off the beaten path.

Her promise of a small but ancient stone circle in the middle of the forest, as yet undiscovered by anthropologists or tour companies or TV producers, had instantly captured Dee's imagination. But it been no match for a cairn dedicated to the glorious dead of the Great War, at least not as far as Brad was concerned. He wanted historical background and cultural significance spelled out on plaques that he could photograph and catalogue. He was researching a new book — something depressing about grief and commemoration in Scotland — and had started seeking out Dee's ancestral lines in the process. Her family had apparently come from this part of Skye, but the connections he'd been seeking had all been uncertain. The possibility of a cairn that might hold the names of some of her ancestors was beyond his wildest hopes. So he had left her, clearly disappointed by her lack of interest in this unexpected genealogical gold mine, but promising to return soon.

"Or as soon as I can," he'd added ruefully, and kissed her. "Between the state of the roads and the feral sheep crossings, it could take all day. Are you sure you want to stay? You won't be bored out of your mind?"

"A stroll through the woods is exactly what I need," she'd said, trying to refrain from pushing him out the door. "I could use a break from the battlefields. All those lost souls..." She'd smiled and let the words fade away to forestall his concern, to disguise her relief. She'd slept poorly the night before, her dreams filled with the echoes of all the haunted places that they had visited. She had awakened to find herself wrapped in a longing for something she could no longer remember as the dream unravelled.

Brad had nodded and kissed her once more, his mind already on his research and the day ahead. She'd laughed silently as he ground the gears of their rental car, imagined him cursing the manual transmission. Dee watched until he turned a bend and was lost from sight.

Auntie had errands to run as well. "I've made you a cup of tea, hen," the old lady had called on her way out the door. "Why don't you take it through to the garden?" Then she, too, had disappeared down the lane with a nod and a wave of the old-fashioned basket she carried.

So here Dee sat, serenaded by crows and wind and leaves, a volume of folklore from Auntie's library unheeded on her lap. She'd stopped reading when she came to the sorrows of her own tragic namesake, wondering for the millionth time what her mother had been thinking when she'd named her.

"I'd been planning to call you Audrey, but when I looked at you…" Her mother had told her this story a thousand times, punctuated by a wave of her hand meant to encompass Dee's entire being.

Dee shook her head and sighed, wondering what kind of life Audrey might have led. She *wasn't* complaining — by all rational methods of accounting, the joys of her life had far outweighed the sorrows — but she couldn't help but feel the name had left her vulnerable to moments of whimsy and melancholy to which the plucky Audrey might have been immune.

She lifted the delicate porcelain cup to her lips, then set it back on its saucer untasted. A spirit of restlessness seized her and she rose, intending to exchange the tattered book for one of the glossy magazines she'd picked up at the airport. Instead, her feet took her to the garden gate. To her disappointment, it was locked. The wind rustled the leaves and the crows jeered. She sought the hecklers in the trees, intending to give them an Audrey-like chiding for their cheek, and noticed a heavy iron key hanging within arm's reach. The key turned in the lock, and a sigh went through the trees. She felt the tension that had gripped her since they'd begun their tour of Scottish battlegrounds begin to dissipate.

She stepped across the threshold from the garden into the forest and took a deep breath. Her senses were instantly flooded by the verdant life around her. She breathed even more deeply, allowing the heady scents and colours to buoy her spirits. She thought with sadness of her husband's solitary journey in his rental car to a place where even the ghosts would be devoured by the voracious appetites of tourists and the bereaved. Another breath and she was overcome by gratitude that she was here rather than there. Alone, for once. For once not lonely. She ignored the knowledge that this was a temporary escape — perhaps she could convince Brad to stay another night or two. Perhaps Auntie knew more local war stories that could claim Brad's attention. Dee crossed her fingers and her face lightened.

She surveyed the path, which split in two directions. Auntie had mentioned that the stone circle was a popular place for locals, particularly the amorous youth, and Dee was relatively certain that the branch that meandered off to her left would take her in the direction of the village

Auntie had indicated. As she took her first step, however, the cries of the crows burst over her; for a moment, she feared that she had strayed too close to a nest and that they would swoop down to drive her away. Heart pounding, she moved back toward the gate. To her relief, the crows quieted. That decided it. She began walking as briskly as she could on the uneven, overgrown path toward the heart of the forest.

"You've got Scottish blood," the old lady had stated, her sharp eyes taking in Dee's hair and face and complexion. "You could be mine own granddaughter."

"Dee's family originated here in the Hebrides," Brad had told Auntie proudly, as though the old woman herself were not rooted in such places. "But you know how it was," he went on, pausing significantly. "The Clearances…"

The old woman had nodded, her smile tolerant. Clearly, she was used to tourists coming in search of connections to a long-lost homeland. Neither seemed to notice how powerfully her words had struck Dee, calling her back into the past.

Dee's curiosity about her heritage had been dampened long ago by memories of her grandmother and mother arguing about how much or how little the ancient past mattered when one was struggling to keep a roof over one's head *right now*. The pressing needs of the present had always taken priority over what her mother had considered flights of fancy. Her grandmother had raged at that phrase, "flights of fancy", insisting to the last on the urgency of remembering. Dee felt long forgotten memories stirring as she stepped deeper into the untouched woods.

Fairy Tales from the Rock 39

From the depths of the past, a rhyme surfaced:

> *Never chase the fox's fire,*
> *Always greet the crows,*
> *Beware the wily messenger,*
> *With caution approach the stones.*

There was more — but she couldn't remember it. Her grandmother had tried to teach Dee the poems and stories she had learned from her own grandmother, and had bitterly lamented Dee's refusal to learn them in their original Gaelic.

"Ciamar a tha thu an-diugh, a ghràidh?" her grandmother had greeted her every morning. *How are you, my dear one?* Dee always refused to answer, insisting that she couldn't understand, and her grandmother would sigh. "You are too stubborn for your own good! Just like your mother."

"*You're* the stubborn one," Dee would tell the old woman, her voice echoing the irritable, world-weary tones of her own mother. "Can't you just let it go?" And Dee would complete the imitation by shaking a finger at the old woman. They would laugh, and the moment would pass. But on the final day, the last time she'd seen her grandmother, the old lady had taken her hand and spoken with quiet insistence.

"My dear one, mine own. The language, the stories, are in your blood and bones, whether you like it or not. Someday you may have cause to remember that. I pray it will all be for the best." She'd sighed and squeezed Dee's hand. "O Uill... Dè ghabhas dèanamh?" *Oh well, what can you do?*

Dee remembered these words with pain, uttered the Gaelic phrase aloud for the first time in more than two decades. The words, spoken barely above a whisper, weighed heavily in the air. How well it encapsulated her life in its entirety.

The argument had been an old one. Dee remembered the first time she had become aware of it — creeping downstairs late at night, seeking comfort after a bad dream, but stopping and listening when she heard raised voices.

"But why would you name her after one of the Folk?"

"First of all, Mother, you know that's complete nonsense," her own mother had scoffed. "I thought you would love that I'd named her after one of your stories. And second, I don't remember ever reading anything that said *she* was one of the Fae."

"You wouldn't have," her grandmother had retorted. "Most of those stories weren't written down. Her father was a harper for the Folk. She was taken from them when a Druid prophesied that her beauty would result in the deaths of warriors and kings."

"That's the story of Helen of Troy." Her mother's laughter had become forced, impatient. "Now, finish your dram and let's call it a night."

Her grandmother had muttered something too quietly for Dee to hear. She wished she could have seen her mother's face but, whatever the expression, those muttered syllables had resulted in the old woman being sent to bed as unceremoniously as Dee herself when she was discovered eavesdropping.

Dee chuckled; she could picture herself as a skinny child, shivering on the stairs, all scraped knees and wide eyes and big ears. She had loved her grandmother's stories, then. It was only later, when her friends at school disabused her of her belief in fairy tales, that she came to resent the stories as her mother did. But before the children's mockery had changed her, the world had been full of wonder — if you knew how to see it.

She and her grandmother had known.

As she walked and remembered, the timbre of the crows' jeers changed. Now, she would swear they seemed almost welcoming. The shadows deepened. She sloughed off the cares she had brought with her like a skin.

The underbrush grew thicker. A thorn scratched a long thin line across her arm. Three scarlet drops welled. *It's in your blood and bones.* How she had blamed the old woman for planting that seed. Nothing could uproot it: not her mother's sarcasm, nor her classmates' casual cruelty, nor her own attempts to do everything correctly, to achieve those things that her mother promised would bring happiness. *An education, a job, a husband, a home.* Instead of happiness, she had reaped only frustration, and a loneliness that nothing in this world could salve.

Still she walked, pushing back branches that snagged her hair and her clothes. She looked up at the sky, but she couldn't see the sun through the thick canopy. She wasn't sure how long she'd been walking — it felt like no time at all, surely not much more than half an hour, but already the daylight seemed to be fading. The thought that she should turn back flickered through her mind, but now she was committed. *Too stubborn for your own good,* she thought.

So she pushed on, breathing the scent of cranberries and promising to turn around if she didn't find the circle in five minutes. In ten minutes. Fifteen minutes, tops.

She burst out of the trees into a clearing just as she meant to surrender to the pull of the life she had temporarily relinquished. She looked again for the sun to gauge the time, but the sky was hazy and distant, the texture of the light unfamiliar. For the first time, she felt unease. Still, she did not turn back.

There were three ancient stones: broken, irregularly spaced, low to the ground. Not the circle that Auntie had mentioned at all. This appeared to be something else entirely. A hearth, perhaps. Maybe a filled well. She took an eager step forward, then hesitated. Her grandmother's warnings about carelessly wandering into places of power brushed her mind like black wings. Even from a distance of several metres, she imagined she could feel the cold breath of the ages pouring out of the ruins. She took another step and startled as a murder of crows launched into the sky. She watched it go, and rued her own earthbound state.

When her gaze again turned to the toppled stones, she was startled to find a large crow standing before her. She stared at it, thought to shoo it away, but it held her with a glittering eye. *If this were one of Gram's stories,* she thought, *I'd introduce myself to this crow, and he would teach me his se-*

crets. Her throat tightened as she swallowed the wanting that had haunted her all her life.

Feeling foolish, Dee dropped a clumsy curtsey and bowed her head to the crow.

"My grandmother sends her greetings, Master Crow," she said, trying to keep her voice light, pretending she was making a joke. "Ciamar a tha thu an-diugh, a ghràidh?"

The crow said nothing for a moment, then croaked once and hopped closer to her. A flurry of feathers disturbed the air behind her as the murder resumed their front-row seats around the clearing.

"It is truly a pleasure to meet you, my dear sir," Dee told him, thrilled by his approach and hamming it up for their audience. "I hope you don't mind if I call you Crow — I've not yet mastered your elegant tongue." She curtsied again.

Another croak, another hop.

"Who am I?" she asked, delighting in the game. "Why, I'm Dee!"

The crow froze as the murder began shouting their derision, then turned his back on her. He gurgled deep in his throat, silencing the others. He seemed poised to fly.

"Wait! Master Crow! Let us play a little longer!" If the crow abandoned her, she would follow the path back to the loves and regrets that would even now be waiting for her. "Don't go! Please, how have I offended?" The crow gave no sign that he had heard her.

"What did I say? My name... was it my name?" Dee took a step closer, then backed away as the crow shuddered. Again, the flutter of dark wings in her mind. A warning. "Forgive me, I haven't introduced myself properly. I'm Deirdre. Deirdre is my name."

The murder exploded into sound, their cacophony drowning out the entire world. The crow turned and drew closer, its eye glittering with fierce delight. *Deirdre.* Her name floated on the wind. For the first time, she felt its power resonate in the core of her being. *Deirdre.*

Unbidden, unstoppable, her hands stretched toward the crow, which hopped fitfully first on one foot then the other. *Never chase the fox's fires.* Fingers lengthened, hands floated of their own accord toward the sky. *Always greet the crows.* Eyes rolled back into the skull, which elongated to form a strong, perfect point. *Beware the wily messenger.* Black wings unfurled and stretched, casting shadows across the clearing. *With caution approach the stones.*

Two crows launched themselves into the sky and were gone.

"Deirdre," the forest whispered. *"A ghràidh. Mine own."*

Isobel Granby

Granby is an author and poet currently living in St. John's. Their previous work includes "The Date-Book," for Queer Sci-Fi "Ink" anthology, "The Second," from the Metapsychosis online journal, "Portrait of a Lady," from the Queer Sci-Fi "Migration" anthology and "The Mark," from Lighthouse Digest. They have been shortlisted or won multiple awards for their work, including the Chatterton 250 Poetry Contest, the 2020 Gregory J. Power Poetry Prize, the 2020 Íslendingadagurinn Open Prose Prize, the 2019 Helen M. Schaible Sonnet Contest, and the 2019 Íslendingadagurinn Open Poetry Prize.

Their work appeared previously in *Acceptance: Stories at the Centre of Us*, a collection in benefit of the Quadrangle charity.

The Riddle-Game

In the blue-grey dawn, the sleeper woke. Despite the clouds, there was a clarity to the air, a gleam that vanished with the onset of day. It was why she had begun rising early: before the sun burned too bright, she could see farther. The moment passed, and she was herself again, stumbling down the stairs, the fleeting melancholy replaced by practical concerns.

"Tea, Miss Morag?"

She nodded gratefully at Aoife, the serving girl, who greeted her with the same question each morning. Each day she rose early, and drank tea at a table by the window, before walking to the village. She had grown fond of the scones. This morning she read as she ate, opening a book of Shakespeare's sonnets from the inn's shelf. The words were like nothing she had known in her own language, but she enjoyed their music all the more for it. A beam of sunlight fell across the page, from the half-open window which let in the morning air.

The postman had waited for her at the road. "Letter

for you."

"Thank you." He nodded, then continued up the road, further from the village. She tore open the envelope and found a slip of plain paper, with a single line of writing.

The game begins tonight at the foot of the mountain.

A game — the writer was teasing her. No, she would not be made sport of by some stranger, some upstart wishing to mock at her ragged state.

A game, indeed; she paused. She had not tried her hand at a game for so long, and if she could win it, she might restore her name.

Seven years she had lived in the human world; seven years since her departure from the islands. In the seventh year of her reign (years were different there), she had longed to see the country from which her own people had been banished. Though many of the older folk told stories of their visits there, they had for a countless span been outcasts from those lands, and to visit them meant exile.

Even as she had sailed there, she had remembered the law. And she had gone to the mainland laughing at it. When she had turned back to look at the islands as she stepped ashore, they were no longer there.

By the old laws, her exile should have lasted a year and a day. She could no longer reckon time in their ways. In this world, a year could be a minute, or it could be a century. She would only know when it ended. It had not been entirely unpleasant. There was music, there was food and wine — the little pleasures of a little world, along with its petty strifes. She had travelled from town to town, along the northern coast. People always did settle near water, and in each place she heard, underlying the hubbub of the street, the rushing murmur of the far-off sea. This latest village was warm and welcoming, and they never doubted her coin, though it returned to her purse each night — one of the few treasures, along with her gift for languages, that she had brought with her. She chose a name with which to endure her exile. She was happy in the company she chose, though she could have no close acquaintance.

Happiness was not satisfaction. The relentless curiosity that had led her here now thrilled at the note in her hand. There was nothing for it but to answer, and if she lost the game, what difference would it make?

A full moon shone above her. The light of it made the shadows around her dance. Far off, she could see white caps on the sea, the sound of the surf seeming to come from across the world.

In her rucksack she had all that she needed to find her way: not only a sparker, and a little tinderbox with which to light the candles she had brought, but an Ordnance Survey map, a compass, and an English guidebook recently written. That would not necessarily help, but it bolstered her courage in the face of the twisting tunnels, the maze-like interior of the mountain. If she did get hopelessly lost, she would at least know the names of every type of rock.

At the mouth of the tunnel, the rocks began to glow faintly, a pale, greenish colour that seemed to deepen the shadows around her. It emanated from the moss that grew there, a gloomy natural phenomenon that prevented most people from delving too far into the mountain. Only one court had moved into it. That had been long ago, before the islanders had been banished from the mainland, and they had faded to a sinister legend among the oldest inhabitants.

"They may not remember me, but I've heard of them all right," she laughed. "I know I'm walking into a trap, and if that's so, I can avoid being caught, can't I?" She was wrong, but it is impossible to explain that to someone intent on walking into a trap.

At last, at the end of the sloping tunnel, her right hand (stretched out ahead, while the other stayed raised in case of ambush) met cold stone. Now she faced a dilemma. If she lit the candle in her rucksack, she risked being detected. The prospect of groping around in the dark for hours was equally unappealing. There was something carved in the stone. She needed a light, something that would allow her to see but stay unseen. Suddenly she remembered the phosphorescent mosses and began moving cautiously back towards the tunnel's mouth.

The mosses, in the blackness of the tunnel, glowed like green coals. The carvings on the stone were letters, she had been right, and by the moss-light, she could make them out. It was an old script, but she read them with ease. It was a request for a password, something like *moonlight*, and she tried several variations on the theme.

"Moonshine, more like," she grumbled. "I can't very well bring the moon itself into the mountain." But even as she said it, she was rushing back up to the mouth of the tunnel and fumbling in her rucksack. How to do it — she had a curved tin shade for the candle — would that be enough? There was a bend in the tunnel, another reflector would be needed — the mirror in the lid of the compass.

Just enough moonlight to work.

She set the shade by the entrance, adjusted the angle, then walked, tracking the ray with her compass mirror, down to the bend in the path. Flashing the pale, trembling beam, barely visible, towards the end of the tunnel, she waited.

The door swung back. No sentry, no guard or welcoming party, appeared. Stepping over the threshold, she entered a new tunnel, this one wider and grander. Moving more confidently, she kept a hand on the wall, but began to look around at the realm she had entered.

The air moved in a faint breeze, and it was warm, but not stiflingly so. The darkness had a rich, velvety quality to it. She could smell earthy scents, not unpleasant, but strong. There was the sound of running water, and the dripping of stalactites. As she made her way along, the walls became smoother, and now and again, her eyes would detect a flash of something within the stone, until she saw that they were veins of gold, running through the rock.

Far ahead, there was a deep, rusty glow. Firelight — and this was all she knew before two figures stepped from the shadows, took her by the arms, and brought her to the hall of the queen.

Her throne was carved from the rock of the mountain. Thin veins of gold entwined themselves in her flowing hair, or rather it seemed that her hair, bright in that black chamber, had grown from the mountain. It was the only crown atop the queen's handsome head.

Morag sank to one knee, her head bowed and her heart pounding. Her black hair fell across her eyes and she did not brush it aside. This rival of hers, this enemy by tradition, a legend whom the islanders had once dreaded, commanded every ounce of her attention.

"You agreed to my terms."

No greeting, Morag noted wryly. Nothing so courteous. "You expected me not to?"

A ripple of low laughter echoed around the hall. The air was too hot to think, and this was the only reason she could give for doing what she did next — she rose from her knee.

The guards on either side moved to their ruler protectively. But she waved them away, smiling at her guest.

"We face each other as equals. Quite right. Now, for the prize — surely you want to know."

In truth, the prize was an afterthought. She wished to know, to win it, less for its own sake than that of the winning. The queen beckoned, and a figure approached. At the sight of his face in the flickering torchlight, she caught her breath. Her own — he was here, against his will, silent in the darkness, in this place where sunlight came not. How he had come there, she could not guess — and this alone made her pause, and doubt.

"How do I know this is no illusion?" She looked away from him, and his eyes full of questions, and did not permit herself to hope.

"Do you think me so petty?"

Her questions made no headway; she was sailing upwind between cliff and reef. Returning the queen's stare, she replied in kind.

"If you are not, how can you have him in your keeping?"

The torches leapt again, seemingly in answer to her impertinence. But the queen's voice, when it came, was choking with laughter, almost more frightening than wrath.

"A bold question!" Her voice dropped to a murmur. "Are you so heedless of your safety?" She leaned forward, her hair catching the torchlight in its waves. "Or did you not think there was any danger in accepting my challenge? Know this, little trespasser, I may lie hidden, forgotten by the world, but there is strength in me yet." The queen rose slightly from her chair, her voice growing menacing. "You will not leave here save by my command. Nor will you take what is mine."

For once, words failed Morag, as she tried to convince herself that she had done right in coming here. She had heard of this queen and her subterranean realm, but she had thirsted for some taste of her previous life, even through the eyes of an enemy. Now, she could not know whether it was her rashness or his own that had brought her consort to this deepest dungeon.

Haltingly, she managed to speak. "He is not yours." But this was an ancient game. This was something she could not alter, even in her reign, a contract between all parties. Unless the golden-haired queen had cheated, the man she loved was here by his own agreement.

"Does that matter? No, your majesty; you know the terms of this contest. In exchange for his leaving, I must have a gift, by the time our court next holds revels." Her eyes glinted with humour. "If by the light of the moon you entered, then by the sun, he will be allowed to leave. But the same trick will not serve you twice, however clever you thought it." In its brazier, the red fire leapt up, streaking the ceiling with ash. "Bring me the sun." Then the torches went out, the queen and her court vanished, and Morag was alone on the mountainside once more.

In the distance, the sea shimmered in the early morning light. Her time in the mountain seemed like a dream, and she stumbled down the mountain path, her head light and her body numb. In the growing dawn the birds were waking, and the sound brought her back to the present. The sun was muted by fog. It was a relief, after the darkness, not to be thrust into the full daylight. She did not want to be reminded of her impossible task. And yet — she must start as soon as possible, or her only chance would be lost.

"All very well, but what am I looking for?" she muttered irascibly. It was at once the most obvious thing, and the most unattainable.

Suddenly, she heard a cry.

Far above her, where the sky was white with cloud, a shape was moving. An enormous shadow — but its voice was piercing and clear, and on hearing it, a sudden hope had sprung up in her heart, and she leapt to her feet. It was an eagle.

"Come down!"

The bird wheeled higher, with another cry. Here was one who knew her true name. Such birds she had seen on the island many times before, and never since leaving had one appeared to her in daylight — only in dreams.

"Come down!"

Lighter than the wind she ran, sliding on the rocks, but never slowing. The bird would soar high, then swoop low, each time further off — yet never out of sight. She tracked its shadow on the rocks, higher and higher up the slope. There was the sea beyond, and the ragged line where it met the shore in shocks of white spray. There, far off, was her own country, and so keenly could she tell where it ought to be that she could almost see it. The eagle had vanished, but as she listened, above the roar of the sea, she could hear its piercing cry. *The eagle knows.*

It could fly to the sun, so her people said, and in its eyes the sunlight itself shone. It would do. She could coax it to her arm, run with it down to the place where the queen waited, certain of victory. Without stopping to think — that would never have helped, anyway — she ran upward, not stopping to catch her breath until her foot slipped on a patch of grass, and in catching her balance, she looked down. The sight made her start in horror. She had followed the eagle to the edge of a precipice, the steep cliff falling away on the other side of the mountain.

Breath and feeling and thought came back at one blow, and she stood reeling. She had a head for heights and a knack for climbing, but this was too much. She had made her usual mistake, rushing headlong into danger instead of persuading the answer to come to her.

This game would call for a different approach. It was paramount that she regain the element of surprise, the only advantage she could claim.

The sky beyond the inn's windows was restless, as she

paced her room. However broadly she searched, and she had walked over road and hill and festering bog every day, she could find no answer to the riddle. Everything was dim and cool; the air, electric. In the silence before the clouds broke, there was time to think without the glare of the sun. Somehow the light made it difficult to think. Somehow it seemed likely that this was the mountain queen's doing.

"What will it be?" she murmured, as the rain drew in like a curtain across the land. "What gift shall I offer you, my queen?" Perhaps this would be her fate, to serve the golden-haired lady forever. To have her love returned to her, both of them silent, prisoners. To live beneath the mountain, and to never see the sea — there she halted, for that thought was too hard to endure.

The task was to be completed by Midsummer, when the court would feast and dance in their subterranean halls. That was a week away. Each day, she woke earlier and more uneasily. Each new search brought forth no answers. At last, there came a time when she could sleep no longer, and breakfasted at dawn, and passed the day as in a fevered dream.

Long into the evening, she would watch the stars and moon until the space between them was filled with the remnants of their light. Now and again, a star fell, and only this disturbed her peace: for all at once it seemed an easy thing, to catch this small sun as it burned through the sky.

It was the day before Midsummer's Eve. The world

had melted into a gold-edged, tyrannical brightness. She turned the riddle over in her mind as she sat in the shade of the inn's garden, but to no avail. Thought followed exhausted thought in no real order, every thread she caught unwinding before she could make any sense of it.

A line entered her mind unbidden. The book she had been reading the day she had opened the letter, the book of verse. *Sometimes too hot the eye of heaven shines.* The eye of heaven was the sun. If the words could suggest an answer to the riddle, she could surprise the queen. But it made no sense. It was too hot to concentrate, too bright to think.

Suddenly she sat bolt upright. Whether it was her sleep-starved state, or the momentary recollection of the poem, something had made sense out of nonsense: there was a patch of flowers swaying just out of her reach, fluttering a little in the breeze. A patch of daisies.

Midsummer's Eve dawned clear as glass. The fine light in the sky was crisscrossed with clouds, gleaming gold in the sun, blown across the blue of evening.

In the hall, the revels had begun. Their music rang through the corridors, into the tunnel beyond, where anyone passing might have heard it and been enchanted, as still happens. The guards' black attire had been replaced by jewel-encrusted garments of all kinds, sparkling gaudily in the torchlight, which made her smirk a little. *Imagine us wearing — or no, please don't.* Her own people had *taste*.

The queen was plainly surprised by her return.

"Happy Midsummer's Eve, your majesty. May I say

what a ... spectacular sight your courtiers make." Morag stood in her drab clothing and with her eyes clouded with weariness, but a grin on her face. "I have returned with the gift that you asked of me."

"Show it, then."

With a flourish, she produced the flower from her pocket, and held it out. "The day's eye, that is, the sun. Just as you requested."

The queen stood at that, and her eyes flashed; for a moment it seemed as though she would strike her guest. Then, just as suddenly, she laughed.

"A game well played!"

It was not over yet, Morag knew. There was always a third riddle. "A board well set," she replied cautiously.

"You solved the riddle of my doorway. That, I'll grant you, was an easy question. The sun, too, you have brought into my chamber, you impudent creature. Now for the last part of our engagement: how do you intend to get out?"

"By what means you allow, my lady," she replied simply.

"This knife" — here she threw Morag a small golden blade — "is the key to your escape. All that you must do is to find the lock. Do that, and his freedom is won, you may both come and go as you will to my court. After all, you have not been exiled from here."

She caught her breath. There were a thousand tunnels through the darkness, some going on forever. She could spend an eternity in search of the lock, and never find it. The knife was a slender little thing, its blade a mere hairsbreadth. And gold, gold as the queen's own hair.

Gold. That was it.

"I have already found it." She could not conceal her excitement. "Any lock that would fit such a key must be of the same material. I do not need to search for such a lock. It is right before me." The queen leaned forward, intrigued. There was no other chance — she lunged, catching the end of one lock of hair. The little knife cut right through, and she took it in one hand, as the other reached out for the touch she had longed for since the beginning of her exile.

At a word from the mountain queen, all of the torches in the hall went out. Thrown into sudden darkness, the islanders could do nothing but reach for each other, holding fast, though all else in the world might disappear. And, indeed, it seemed that it had: the golden-haired lady, her guards, and the whole subterranean court had vanished into thin air.

"Let's be off."

It was the first time in seven human years that she had heard his voice.

"Please." She trusted herself with one word only. They walked in silence, their hands the only bond between them. It was enough.

Once in the open air, she asked, "Where will you take passage?" Her voice sounded different, she realised suddenly, on hearing his. A difference in accent, slight but there.

"With you," he answered, not understanding. "We return together."

But she shook her head, her eyes meeting his levelly. "The game was for your freedom, not my return. Why did you agree to play her game?"

He turned to her, taking both of her hands in his. "Why did you?"

She took his point. "It has been so long."

"I thought it would permit you to return. I failed."

"No. You risked everything." She felt her heart hammering. "The terms of my exile were clear. A year and a day, and then, who knows?" But it did not seem so lonely, now, to say it aloud to him, whom she had never thought to see here, on the banks of the sea.

"You will return. And until then, I will tell your story, so that you will return a hero. They will speak your name with admiration." He kissed her hand, bending slightly towards her. "I swear it to you." Dawn turned the sea to gold as they watched the horizon, and for a brief moment, which could have been mistaken for a dream, she saw the islands once more.

Stacey Oakley

Stacey Oakley is an author originally from Moncton, New Brunswick who became a vibrant part of the local Newfoundland writing scene after the publication of "The Sorrows of War" in the 2016 edition of *Sci-Fi from the Rock*.

She has since gone on to independently publish her own novel, *Hunter's Soul*, its follow up *The Necromancer*, and in 2018 was crowned the winner of the 48 Hour Novel-Writing Marathon.

Wolves in the Woods

Once upon a time, there was a town near the edge of the forest. The town was surrounded by a thick wall, and those who lived there never ventured beyond the wall at night, and never went into the forest at all if it could be avoided. If it weren't for the trade route that passed through, the town would have vanished long ago, its people scattered to safer places.

Only the experienced woodsmen dared brave the woods, or a hunter when prey was scarce. Occasionally visitors would venture forth, lured in by the tales told by the safety of the firelight, or youths would try to prove their foolish courage. Once in a while, when a child was taken, a heartbroken parent would make a desperate attempt at rescue. The most they would ever find was a scrap of cloth, and nothing more. The wolf's tracks would always lead to a dead end.

But there hadn't been wolves in the region for as long as anyone could remember. They had been hunted and driven out long ago in an attempt to save the townspeople. But the disappearances never stopped, and all signs would point to a wolf as the culprit, no matter how closely the guards watched from the wall.

Those who survived the woods sometimes spoke of an eerie laughter among the trees, seeing a flutter of cloth between the trees and out of the corner of their eye. The woodsmen and hunters would shudder at the mention of it and end any conversation. Once in a while, a brave knight would pass through and try their hand at solving the mystery and saving the town. Their armour would be found at the edge of the woods later, bloody and covered in deep claw marks.

One day, a young man came to the village. He had been sent by the father of his intended, to kill one of the fabled wolves and bring back its pelt to prove he was worthy of marrying the woman he loved. In truth, the son of a nobleman had objected to the match, wanting to marry the young woman himself. Her father, hoping to avoid a duel, sent the young man so he could prove himself a hero and the nobleman's son wouldn't dare try to ruin the couple's happy ending. While the young man was not rich, he was skilled, and his ability to wield a sword made him confident he could succeed against a mere wolf.

The young man listened to all the tales the townspeople were willing to tell, and ventured forward one cold morning at dawn, his own father's sword at his side, and enough supplies to last a week.

For a day and a half he wandered, before he heard laughter in the distance, the giggle of a child at play. He followed the sound, wary, and discovered a young girl in a red riding hood picking wildflowers.

"Are you lost?" he asked the child, wondering if this was one of the children from the town that had vanished.

"You're a long way from town." And there was no other town or village for at least two days' travel.

She smiled and skipped over to him, a basket on one arm. "I'm going to visit my grandmother, who is sick. I thought she might like some wildflowers. She isn't far from here. Will you walk with me? My mother says there are wolves in the woods, and I must be careful and not stray from the path..." Her lower lip trembled slightly. "She won't be happy that I have, but I just wanted to help my grandmother feel well again."

Thinking that perhaps there could be another village that the townspeople were ignorant of out of fear, the young man nodded. "There are dangerous wolves in these woods. Is your grandmother far from here?" He felt a need to help the child, who looked so bright and innocent. He didn't want any harm to befall her. So, he followed as she started walking, leading him deeper into the woods.

"A little far," she replied. "My mother would normally come with me, but she says I am grown enough now, and she must mind my younger brothers and sisters. They are too young to walk on their own."

"You must be proud she has such faith in you," he said.

"I am," she replied. "But not too proud. That would be bad. Mother says too much pride is a bad thing in a person."

"Your mother sounds wise," he agreed. He didn't know how long they had been walking, and was growing tired, though the girl seemed to have just as much energy as when they'd started.

"Your pack and sword must be heavy," the girl in the red riding hood said a little while later. "Why don't you put them down and come back for them later?"

"But I need my sword, in case we meet a wolf," he replied. But the girl was right, it was very heavy. "Perhaps we could sit for a moment."

"Yes," the girl said. "Oh, I know the perfect place. My grandmother showed it to me, there is a spring that we could drink from."

The young man realized he was thirsty and nodded in agreement, following the girl. They soon reached a clear stream with banks lined by a thick moss and plants with towers of purple flowers.

"Drink from the stream," the girl said, sitting down on a rock. "It will restore your strength, and more."

The young man nodded and knelt at the edge of the stream, cupping his hands to drink the cold water. It was refreshing, so much so that he drank more and soon he removed his pack and sword so he could bend over, lapping directly from the spring. His energy returned, and more. When he lifted his head, a wolf's face stared back. He jumped back and reached for the sword, only to find that his hands had turned into paws.

He was the wolf.

He looked over at the girl, who smiled.

"There are wolves in the woods," she said. "Just like I told you. Now stand and follow me."

The young man found he was powerless to anything but obey, lopping over to her side as she turned and led the way back to the village.

"I do hope you'll do better than the last wolf," the girl

said. "He tried to bite me. Grandmother said he must have been hungry, so when he slept, we filled his belly with rocks. When he woke up, he went to take a drink of water and drowned. Poor thing." She giggled as she skipped through the woods. "The baby he brought Grandmother kept her fed for a while, though. So at least he did that right."

The young man fell into despair, with no idea how he would escape this fate or return to his beloved.

A few weeks passed, and a young woman came to the town accompanied by her sister, searching for her beloved. The townspeople had seen no sign of the traveler. Most had forgotten about him in the face of a new string of children vanishing. Two had been taken in the past month. Much like her lover, she was not without skills of her own. Her father had once rescued her mother from a wicked witch's grasp, and they wanted to ensure that the same fate never befell their children. Both young women wore silver pendants made from treasure taken from the witch who had kept their mother captive, the precious metal a guard against evil and magic.

As prepared as they could be, the two young women ventured into the woods. When the wolf tracks ended, they knew they were on the right path because of the mournful howl they could hear once in a while, especially at night. The young, love-filled woman felt there was something familiar in the sound, though she was not certain what it was.

Two days later, deep in the woods, they heard a child's

laughter. Warily, they followed the sound. Could it be a missing child that escaped? Or something more sinister?

They emerged into a clearing to find a young girl picking wildflowers, a red cape hanging from her shoulders. She looked over and smiled, her expression innocent and almost angelic. The air around her felt strange, like something was trying to draw them in closer.

"Are you lost?" the young woman asked. She and her sister stopped before they got too close to the child. A child alone in the woods should be afraid, not laughing and picking flowers without care.

The girl looked at them with open curiosity even as she answered. "I'm going to visit my grandmother. She is unwell and I am bringing her some things that Mother says will help." She held up a basket for them to see. "I thought she would like some flowers too. They would make her smile, and Mother says it is good to smile." Her expression invited them to share in her joy, to get closer, but they kept their distance.

"You're a long way from the town," the young woman said.

"There is a village not far from here, and my grandmother lives less far still." She frowned. "Mother will not be happy that I strayed from the path, but I truly think these flowers will make Grandmother smile." She looked around. "Mother says there are wolves in the woods, would you walk with me?"

"Your mother says there are wolves, but allows you to walk alone?" the young woman's sister asked.

The girl's frown deepened. "She is busy with my brothers and sisters and has decided that I am old enough

Fairy Tales from the Rock 67

to walk alone." There was pride in her voice, but something didn't sound right.

"Do you walk alone often?" the young woman asked. "We are looking for someone, a young man who would have passed this way a few weeks ago."

The girl smiled once more. "Yes, I met him. He was most kind and walked with me to my grandmother's home."

"Where is he now? He was here to hunt a wolf."

"Follow me, I can take you to him." She started skipping away before either of the young women could say anything. With mixed hope and fear, the young woman and her sister followed, watching for any signs of danger.

"How long do you think it will be before we arrive?" the young woman asked.

"Not long," the girl replied. "Are you thirsty? I know of a stream we could drink from. Grandmother showed me where it is. The water is very good."

"No," the young woman replied. "Let us keep going."

But the girl didn't move. "Are you certain? You have been walking for a long time."

"We have water with us," the young woman's sister replied. "If we are not that far, we will certainly not run out." The girl looked displeased with the answer. "Is something wrong?"

Her expression changed, and she smiled once more. "No, it is just rare that someone does not want to see the stream."

"Perhaps they did not have such an urgent mission,"

the young woman replied. "Shall we continue?"

"Very well," the girl agreed, and turned, walking instead of skipping. The young woman looked over at her sister, who had the same expression of concern. Curious, she removed the silver pendant and handed it to her sister while the girl looked ahead. She felt an immediate pull toward the child, like she wanted to do anything to keep her smiling and safe. Something must have shown in her expression, because her sister lunged to put the pendant back around her neck. The sensation disappeared. They both stopped walking.

"What have you done with my lover?" the young woman demanded, hand going to her side and the sword she carried. Her sister stepped away to give her space and readied to draw her own sword. "What are you trying to do to us?"

The girl turned around, and the innocent façade was gone, replaced by an impish smile to match the menace in her gaze as a lone wolf howled. "If you come to the stream, I will show you." She tilted her head slightly, the movement like a bird, or a wolf. "Though I would like to know why my magic works not on you?"

"Show us this stream, and then we will tell you." The young woman hoped the being's curiosity would help keep them alive. She was proven right when the girl nodded in easy agreement and resumed walking. The sisters both kept their hands on their swords, ready to draw at a moment's notice.

They reached the stream quickly, and stopped when they spotted the wolf drinking from the water. The young woman spotted her lover's sword and pack and started to fear the worst.

"Now," the girl said, "how are you resisting my magic?"

The young woman held up the pendant. "Silver," she replied. "From a witch's hoard. Where is my lover? Have you killed him?"

The girl smiled, too wide for her face, her teeth suddenly much sharper. "You don't recognize him? How sad."

"What?"

The girl waved at the wolf. "Come closer, maybe she'll know who you are then." The beast stepped toward them slowly, with none of his kin's usual grace. It looked like he was struggling against an unseen force. It reached the girl's side when the young woman noticed its eyes. They were not the normal yellow of a wolf. They were the same colour of the eyes she'd looked into so many times and had hoped to spend the rest of her life seeing.

Her sister caught on in the same moment. "How?"

"Does it matter?" I girl asked. "You may not be children, but Grandmother will still be happy for a fresh meal." She looked at the wolf. "Bring them to me."

The young woman didn't know how it came to be, but she knew now how the wolves kept getting past the guards. Animals they might be, but they had the minds and knowledge of humans, and the girl could use it at will. She took a step back, trying to gain a little distance while she tried to formulate a plan. She was familiar enough with some magic, but by no means able to use it, and she was a capable fighter, but not a warrior, and she did not want to harm the man she loved.

She ran out of time when he lost the battle against the command and lunged. He crashed into her sister first, knocking her down and landing in a tangle of limbs and fur. As he had been commanded to catch and not kill, he didn't bite at her throat. The young woman hoped that something else her mother told her about some magical creatures would hold true against this being as her sister removed her pendant and put it around the wolf's neck. He stilled, now pinning her sister to keep her away from the girl, and the girl snarled.

"He's still my creature," she hissed.

The young woman stepped toward her. "What would it take to get him back?"

"You remove that necklace and you drink from the stream and serve me willingly for the rest of your days," she replied. "You will take the young and bring them to Grandmother so that we may feast upon them."

The young woman decided to take another chance. "Would you like the pendant? As I said, it came from the hoard of a great witch."

The girl tilted her head again and considered. "Put your sword on the ground and bring me the pendant."

Both the wolf and her sister protested. While she was no longer protected, it seemed she wasn't quite under the creature's spell yet. The young woman ignored them and set her sword on the ground before walking over the girl. Once she was close, she removed the pendant and held it out. Thought she was braced for the pull of the girl's strange power, it was still nearly overwhelming. The girl smiled that wide, sharp grin as she took it, her gaze focused on the pendant as the young woman drew her dagger and slashed the girl's throat. Blood as bright as her cape spilled, hissing against the iron of the blade. She grabbed her lover's sword as the girl stumbled back and fell, and cut her head off to ensure she was truly dead. The stream, with its strange moss and flowers, vanished, leaving a dry patch of rock, and when she turned around, she saw that her lover was human once more, and they ran into each other's arms, crying with joy.

With the evil defeated, the town began to thrive as it no longer lived in fear, and the young couple stayed while her sister returned home to find her own adventure. Her sister brought with her the tale of the young woman's bravery and skill, and tith the nobleman's son too afraid of her to demand her for a bride, the couple lived happily ever after.

Melissa Bishop

Born and raised in the Mount Pearl area, Bishop is a newcomer to the genre fiction scene in Atlantic Canada whose fantastic prose has taken the provinces community by storm. Her work won three Kit Sora awards: July 2019 'Cycles,' September 2019 'Huntress of the Woods,' and May 2020 'Brightest and Best.' In addition she has placed numerous other times.

Writing about her story 'The Photograph' in *Pulp Science-Fiction from the Rock*, R. Graeme Cameron of Amazing Stories wrote: "This is a classic SF tale... Possibly a reminder that things aren't always what they seem."

Bishop describes herself as a loyal Tolkien fan who enjoyed reading about different mythologies as a child. She currently works as a high school teacher, teaching at the same high school she attended in her youth. She started writing when she was very young and honed her skills in high school, when she started a pen pal friendship that has lasted for over 17 years, writing stories back and forth to each other.

In May 2023 she released her first novel, *The Fairies of Foggy Island*.

The Sleeping Giant of Conception Bay South

Isaac tore down the dirt path, feeling the machine tremble underneath him as it blared over the uneven terrain. He gripped the handlebars hard, twisting the throttle and easing his grip on the clutch. The dirt bike's purr leapt to a roar as it drove faster down the path fenced in by a dense forest. Birds scattered at the rumbling of his machine. Squirrels scurried from the bushes, barely escaping a grim fate under the grind of the tires. Isaac's eyes were intent upon the road, whipping the bike round each bend with precision. He took a moment to feel the wind rushing past him, clinging to his clothes.

The path obscure and the hour early, Isaac found himself the sole rider in the dawning day. Most fourteen-year-olds preferred sleeping in during their summer vacation, but not Isaac. He preferred speed and seclusion on the forest trails to slumber. It meant he did not have to slow down or share the road. He liked that.

He revved the bike as the trail began a steady incline up the hillside. Shifting down a gear, the tires dug deeper into the dirt. The sound startled a creature nearby, rustling the woodland brush on the boy's right. Isaac glanced to see a blur of rusty red fur as his bike zipped by. Were it not for the strange colour amidst the greenery, Isaac would not have seen the fox. The creature had been clever enough to avoid the road, so Isaac sped off on his journey to explore the hilltop.

The small road rose steadily upwards. The land began to level off, the evergreens lining the path breaking away abruptly to reveal a small clearing open to the sky. The ground was rock, leaving little space for any tree to grow. The boy had found this hideaway a few days before and he thought the place rather interesting. Not for the view, which spanned over the rolling hills all the way to the sea, but for the strange hole in the centre of the clearing.

The pit was deep, that was all that Isaac could tell. Its darkness descended to unknown depths as one peered into it. It was perfectly circular, giving it the appearance of a natural well carved in stone. It was a curious thing to find, and Isaac was a curious kid.

Leaving his bike to lie at the edge of the clearing, Isaac pulled off his helmet and tossed it aside. He bent down and scooped up a rock. Standing at the lip of the hole, he hurled the rock into the pit. It bounced back and forth against the granite walls before disappearing into the abyss. Isaac listened to see if he could hear the rock hit the bottom, but only heard it echo on and on. The boy's eyes searched the ground again, looking for something larger to throw this time.

"I wouldn't do that if I were you," a voice called from behind him. Startled, Isaac whipped around and found only the small fox he had passed before. The boy's blue gaze scanned over the woods. No one else was there.

Fairy Tales from the Rock 75

Assuming it to be simply his imagination, Isaac turned back to the fox, stooping down to grab a sharp stone.

"Shoo!" the boy shouted, whipping his arm, and sailing a rock towards the creature. The fox darted back into the brush, disappearing into the foliage that encircled the edges of the clearing. Alone once again, Isaac turned his attention back to the strange hole. He picked up another stone, this one the size of his fist, and flung it down the shadowy chasm. He listened as the rock ricocheted against the walls, clattering all the way down into the unknown. Grinning, the boy was about to gather more things to throw when he spotted black paws perched upon the crevice's ledge. Clutching his hand around another small stone, Isaac made to throw it again in the fox's direction. His hand halted midair as he heard the creature sigh.

"Well, you've gone and done it," the fox said, shaking its head at the black hole. "It'll certainly wake now. Centuries asleep and a foolish boy like you will be the one to wake it."

Isaac staggered back a step or two, eyes wide on the fox.

"Did... did you just talk?" the boy stammered.

The fox's eyes surveyed its surroundings, its head twisting left, then right before settling its gaze back on the boy. "Do you see anyone else?"

Blinking his bright eyes, Isaac shook his head, chestnut hair dancing in the air.

"I must be imagining things." He chuckled to himself, beginning to think he should have slept in.

The fox tilted its head. "Actually, my opinion is that the more recent generations of humans don't imagine enough." Its bushy red tail swept over the dirt behind it. "There was a time when your folk wouldn't dare trek so deep into the woods, with fairies and monsters and all sorts of things about. But the past few decades have made your lot bold. Now you, and at least fifty percent of the population of Conception Bay South, will pay for it."

"What do you mean by that? Wait." The boy stopped himself before he spoke further. "I'm not going to talk to a fox! Foxes don't talk!" He threw the rock in hopes of again scaring off the creature.

The wild thing easily sidestepped the attack.

"See what I mean? No imagination." The fox shook its head. "And I bet you don't believe in giants either? And you, about to wake one and crush half of your little town in the process."

"What are you talking about?!"

"You're standing on the head of a giant, little human. You're throwing rocks down its eardrum. You've never noticed the sweep of the hills here — where they dip and where they don't? Can't you see the silhouette of its sleeping side?" The fox inclined its head to the view, which swept towards the sea. "You don't, do you?" It let out another sigh. "Why do I even bother?"

"A giant?" The boy's tone still held skepticism, but even this was slowly starting to fade. He was talking to a fox, after all.

"Yes. Centuries ago, all the giants of the world fell asleep. Grass and trees, moss and meadow grew over them. They faded into fairy tales and humans forgot about them. Now all the tearing and digging and drilling is causing them to stir. An increase in earthquakes over the last few years, yeah? Tectonic plates shifting?" The fox scoffed. "My whiskers. Your lot are waking the giants."

"We don't have earthquakes in Newfoundland!"

"Newfoundland doesn't have many giants on it," the fox returned. "You're standing on one though, and if you keep this up—" the creature motioned to the pit in the ground. "Then you're going to get a rude awakening very soon. In fact, I think it's already too late. I can sense it stirring. Only a matter of time now."

"You're wrong," Isaac argued, his tone not as certain as it should have been. "There are no giants, and I'm not going to wake one! They don't exist!"

"Oh, and I'm sure you talk to foxes all the time?" The creature raised its brows, turning its nose up at the boy. "Well, fine. Don't believe me. I'll just be on my way. Gotta get far from the danger zone, after all." It began to move to the forest. "I'll have to make a new den, but when the giant settles again, I figure a few places will open up."

Isaac's eyes went wide. "Wait!" he called out. "Okay, okay! I believe you!" He took a step towards the fox, who looked back at the boy. Having gotten the fox's attention, Isaac's tone turned to a hush, his eyes drifting to the enormous eardrum, "What… is there anything I can do to keep the giant asleep?"

"It'll be hard. The giant's waking already. It's subtle right now, but it'll get worse." The fox paused, thinking hard. "But you know, there are a few things we could try to soothe the beast. Impossible tasks for a meager fox like me, but a brave boy like you? Possible, I suppose."

"What will I have to do?"

"Let's start with the most pressing." The fox moved

towards the trees. "Come along, little human."

Through the pathless woods they went. It was crammed with undergrowth that whipped at Isaac's skin and slapped against his face as he pushed his way through the thicket. Ten minutes felt like an eternity to the boy, for the journey grew steeper as the ground dipped down. Wishing he had worn better boots, Isaac trudged along after the fox, soon coming to stand before the gaping mouth of a great cave. The wind seemed to whistle ominously through the crag, like the sound of someone snoring. This sent a chill straight through Isaac.

The fox sat back on its hind legs next to a pile of toppled trees that blocked the cave's entrance. "A group of kids not much older than you left these right in front of the giant's mouth.

Building some hideout or another — a risky endeavor, unless one wants to get swallowed by a giant's snore. And what if the monster sucks a tree in? Or several? They'll get stuck in its throat and lead to one rude awakening. A sleeping giant is dangerous enough; but an angry one? We might lose the whole town then."

"…Okay." Isaac said warily. "So you want me to move the trees?"

The fox nodded.

Isaac took a step forward, looking uneasily towards the shadowy cave. "And the giant won't suck me in with a snore? I'll be okay standing here?"

"I think you'll be alright," the fox speculated, perking its ear as the wind moaned in the

Cave. "Not yet at least. But I wouldn't dally." There was enough uncertainty in the fox's response to send

Fairy Tales from the Rock 79

Isaac straight to task.

The creature turned to leave the boy behind. "When you're finished, I'll meet you on the hilltop."

Isaac never worked so hard or so fast in his life and still the job was arduous. His day drifted on in sweat, his arms straining as he moved the felled debris from the sleeping monster's mouth. Muscles burned with every lift and pull, beads of perspiration building along his brow as he toiled. Without the blare of his bike, the forest became far more ominous. He jumped at a crow's caw from the branches above him and tensed at any rustle in the brush. Each breath from the beast made the boy work harder, fearing he would be swallowed alive at any instant.

The sun shifted in the sky overhead, dipping below the hillside before Isaac was done. Bruised and sore, the boy blundered his way back to the giant's eardrum, where the fox was waiting.

"Done?" the fox asked, sweeping its tail once more.

Isaac gave a nod as he bent over, resting his hands on his knees. He was still catching his breath from the uphill climb through the bramble.

The fox, seeing the boy's struggle, nodded approvingly, then pressed its ear to the earth. "The giant seems to be breathing easier, but we'll have to give it a night. Come back tomorrow and see if the giant will stay asleep."

Isaac's body ached too much to argue and with a grim nod he moved to take up his dirt bike again.

"Not so loud on that thing this time," the fox added, eyeing the machine. "We don't want all your hard work to go to waste, do we?"

The boy puttered home on his bike as quietly as he

could. The forest path, growing darker now in the fading light, felt far more foreboding than Isaac ever remembered.

The next day dawned without the destruction of Isaac's town. It was with reluctance that the boy traveled the quiet morning path to meet with the fox. He wanted this adventure over with. For surely, he had stopped the giant from waking? Surely his home was safe once more?

The fox did not think so.

With its ear pressed to the rock, the animal let out a deep sigh. "It's still stirring," the fox said solemnly. "We haven't settled it completely. It may yet wake up."

Isaac frowned, crestfallen. His shoulders slumped at the unfortunate news. "What are we going to do?" There was dismay in Isaac's voice.

"Fear not, little human," the fox assured. "I may have just the idea to help calm the giant."

Through the forest they trekked again, Isaac stumbling after the surefooted fox until they came to a small stream nestled near the giant's eardrum. It was only a trickling thing, hardly noticeable save for the outline of small stones set on its banks. The fox stopped at a spot where the stream swelled, almost rising over its sides. A black paw pointed to where the water spilled over haphazardly. "So much garbage has flowed down this stream over the years and it always gets stuck here. Now the waterway is a shadow of itself. Once upon a time, its sweet sound would help the giant sleep. It is calming to the monster's ears and may send it back to slumber if we can get the river going again."

"How do we do that?" Isaac asked, grimacing at the grimy garbage blockading the water's path.

The fox scooped its paw beneath the stream's surface and swung it upwards, knocking a tin can onto the grass between them. "Clean up the river."

"Ew, I'm not touching all that junk!"

"Alright then," the fox replied with a flick of its tail. "Then I suppose we'll just let the giant wake?"

Isaac was about to protest but the words caught in his throat. He envisioned his family and friends under the shadow of the sleeping colossus. "Fine," the boy grumbled, bending to pick up the can. It was slimy under his fingertips, making the boy squirm. He wondered how long the metal thing had lain in the murky mud of the stream's bed. With a wince, Isaac took his knapsack from his back and unzipped it, tossing the trash inside.

The fox seemed pleased. "A good lad. Now when your task is done, meet me on the hilltop and see if our plan has worked."

The afternoon was as laborious as the day before. The summer heat lay heavy on the forest of thin, spindly pines. Isaac found reprieve in sweeping his hands through the cool waters as he searched the dam for debris. It was unpleasant work, but as the young boy toiled, the water began to flow more freely. The trickling of its descent down the hill grew as Isaac plucked more from its muddy bed. The sound drifted into the air, disturbed occasionally by the chatter of a squirrel and, at one point, the croak of a crow perched upon a nearby branch. It seemed to watch Isaac work for a time before flying off again. In this way the boy labored long into the day.

When his task was done, Isaac made his way to the giant's ear, the echo of the stream trailing behind him.

"Excellent, little lad!" the fox said as the boy came into view. It bent its ear low to the earth once more and listened. The stillness of the wilderness settled between them as Isaac watched with eager eyes.

A moment passed in silence before the fox raised its head and spoke. "I think this might have worked. You can hear the little river now, so let's give it one more night. Return to me tomorrow. We shall see if the monster sleeps."

The third day rose. Isaac decided to leave his bike behind and hike the woods by foot. In the early morning hour the forest stirred with waking wildlife. For the first time since Isaac could remember, he heard the soft chirp of birds calling the world awake. He noted the sound of scuttling things in the bushes beside him, and felt the wind tussle his hair under its own strength, not forced by the speed of Isaac's machine. A calm washed over him as the ground beneath his feet rose. He could hear once more the stream's tinkling melody guiding him to the hilltop.

As he ascended to the giant's head, he found the fox waiting for him. "No machine today? Good, we just got the giant settled. Would hate to wake it up again."

"Then it's back to sleep?" Isaac's eyes lit up brightly as the question fell from his lips.

The fox nodded. "Yep. I've checked several times since the sunrise. Congratulations kid, you just saved Conception Bay South, and I imagine a great deal more."

A smile burst across the boy's face as visions of fairy tale heroes flashed in his mind. He had done it! Little Isaac, just fourteen years old and the hero of his hometown!

"Then that's it? I can go home? It won't wake anymore?"

"Well, there's one more thing we can do to make sure this never happens again," the fox said.

"Anything!" Isaac shouted, then hurriedly hushed his voice as if his elation might make their triumph turn sour. "What do we have to do?"

"Follow me, I'll show you."

For the final time, the boy followed the fox through the forest, stumbling here and there but his steps more certain than days before. They dipped and rose over the hills until both stood at a height that Isaac estimated might be the sleeping giant's shoulder. A boulder stood at the top, teetering along the edge, staring out over the expanse like a sentinel on watch. The fox sat beside it, looking once more at the little hero. "We need to block the path," the fox explained, gesturing to the forest below them, "so others of your kind do not make the same mistake you did."

Squinting, Isaac could see the trail snaking through the trees below. He nodded, knowing what he had to do. "The noise won't wake it?" Isaac asked.

"We're fairly far from the ear. Where it's just drifted back to sleep, I don't think this will disturb it," the fox assured.

The lad nodded his agreement — for the fox had led him this far. Thus began the final task on Isaac's quest to settle a sleeping giant.

The boulder was larger than the boy, but not an immovable object for a child his age. He pressed his palms into the stone's rough, uneven surface. Muscles tensed as he pushed against the mound of rock. His arms began to burn as the boy grit his teeth. Bit by bit, Isaac could feel the foundation of the boulder shift and turn on its perch. It leaned a little closer to the ledge, wobbling there for a moment before tumbling to the path below in a thunderous crash. Isaac stood, listening intently as the forest stirred then settled after the commotion of cascading debris. He and the fox remained for a time in silence while the boy caught his breath.

"It's done then?" Isaac asked, breaking the quiet air between them.

The fox nodded stoically. "It's done."

Isaac kept his eyes on the green expanse laid out before them. He listened to a chorus of birds, watched the wind as it rustled the trees, causing them to sway rhythmically.

"So I guess I'll go home," Isaac said after a while, surprised to find himself sad at the adventure's end. He turned to the fox. "Listen… thanks for your help. I'd have awakened the giant if it wasn't for you."

"Don't mention it," the fox returned, bowing its head towards Isaac. "Just remember the sleeping giant whenever you walk the woods. We would not want to disturb it again."

"Goodbye, Fox."

"Goodbye, brave little lad."

The fox watched him go off into the woods below until Isaac disappeared from sight. For a while, the fox merely watched the sun stretch itself across the sky, casting its

Fairy Tales from the Rock

orange glow over the land. The machines still echoed through the forest as the day went on and other humans woke the woods with their noise. But these were merely whispers now, far and away from the fox.

Some time later, long after Isaac had gone, the caw of a crow echoed from above. Black feathers swept from the sky and settled on a stubby pine near where the fox still sat.

"Fox," the creature cooed, tilting its head at the rusty red being. "How did you get the little human to do all that work? Three days the child returned to you and three days he worked to your will. Now the forest is quieter than it was before. The stream we feared drinking from runs clear and smooth. It is all the boy's doing. Why would he work with such speed and strength? For what purpose?"

The fox took a moment to reply, staring out over the land. "I told him he was waking the sleeping giant of C.B.S. His tasks helped send the beast back to sleep," the fox explained.

The crow ruffled its feathers. "But, fox, there are no giants in C.B.S, sleeping or otherwise. I don't think there's a single giant on the entire island, not as far as I have flown, and I have flown over most of it."

The fox's black lips turned upwards into a great grin, showing a gleaming row of teeth. "Oh, I know that," the fox snickered. "But that foolish brat won't be back anytime soon, or any of his kind for that matter." Fox nodded to where the boulder now lay, obstructing the path as if the road had never existed at all. Smirking still, the sly creature turned toward the woods, twisting its tail in triumph. "Now, if you'll excuse me, I have a cave I need to look into. I think it'll make the perfect den."

Ryan Belbin

Ryan Belbin is an author from Pasadena, Newfoundland, whose previous writing credits include "Cause and Effect" for *Paragon III* and "Summer Memories" for *Grenfell Inkpot*.

Previously his work appeared in *Dystopia from the Rock* with the tale "Matches."

Ryan says that, before getting a job where he has to wear ties and tuck in his shirt, he spent a seven month stint hitchhiking across New Zealand.

Bedtime Stories

Once upon a time, there was a husband, a wife, and their son, and they lived a perfectly fine life in a perfectly fine woods, just on the outskirts of a perfectly fine little village. Perfectly fine had been exactly that — until, all of sudden, it wasn't.

It all started, as far as I can tell, when the husband was away in the village, where he worked at the lumber mill, and the son was away visiting his grandparents who lived on the other side of the mountains. The wife, who had always stayed close to the house when the little boy had to be watched near constantly, was able to pack a picnic and head down along the brook, to a clearing, to enjoy the sunshine. However, the beautiful clearing from her memory had become overgrown with brambles and scraggly trees, and all the grass was dead because the sun couldn't get through. A group of witches had taken up temporary residence there (having been banished from most of the civilized parts of the kingdom by that time, they were forced to wander through the darker places), but the wife didn't realize who they were until it was too late.

Or maybe, just maybe, she recognized them immediately, and that was the exact moment she decided to toss perfectly fine to the wind and burn everything else with it. It really doesn't matter anymore; the important thing is, from that day onwards, she started going there much more often. Even when the little boy came home from his trip away, she still found time, when he would go for an afternoon nap, to hurry to the spot where the witches gathered, and sit with them for longer and longer each time, listening to their stories and, ever so slowly, learning their spells to wilt flowers and turn clear water murky. She never spoke of any of this to her husband.

Witches? That's a bit on the nose . . . but fine, the wife went to sit with the witches every so often and, God forbid, have someone to talk to about things other than pulpwood. They weren't like the wart-infested, cackling crones in the storybooks — they liked to laugh but rarely at other's expense, and they were kind to the wife. Meanwhile, the husband started staying out later in the village, after his shift at the mill ended, longer and longer each time. The path through the woods was straight as an arrow, and yet any time there was any mud on the trail (which wasn't infrequently: it rarely rained on the other side of the mountain, where the wife grew up, but the husband had wanted to move the family here and that was that, even though the weather here was far more temperamental), it was obvious that his footprints veered like a cursive loop. He took to kissing his wife and son on the cheeks more, so that they couldn't smell his breath.

The husband believed, especially on those late, *late*

nights in the village, that the witches taught the wife a spell that turned her ugly and wicked. In truth, he couldn't see that what he perceived as ugliness and wickedness developed gradually over many years, often because of the little incantations that he said, perhaps without realizing the dark magic in his speech. His spells were a far more ancient type of dark magic, accidentally passed down through families, but even though he came by it honestly enough, there was a time when he could have unlearned it. The trouble is, like most things that the husband could have done, he just didn't bother, and the dark magic hung over the house. You hear "can't you do anything right?" a few too many times, and you start to believe it — therein lay its sinister power.

It was the witches who introduced the wife to the traveling bard.

The traveling bard was the breaking point. The husband, who woke up at sunrise and trudged off through the forest to a thankless job, all so that he could keep a roof over his family's head and food on the table, came home exhausted one night, to find the oven cold and empty, and a note on the table saying the little boy was spending the night with one of the other families a little deeper in the woods, and the wife would be out late.

Don't wait up, the note ended.

The plate that he maybe tossed to the table a little roughly (because he was tired and misjudged the distance) broke on the floor, and so did the mug. They had been talking about replacing those old things anyway.

The wife was out very late indeed, but the husband had decided to stay up anyway. He was worried about what she did with the witches, what wicked things they taught her, and one look at her when she slipped in through the door confirmed for him that everything that had been perfectly fine about their lives was slipping away, soon to be irretrievable. Everything he did after that was to save her, and to protect his family. That was why he did everything he did.

It had been a beautiful August night, the kind of night where the humidity of the day disappeared and left a pleasant heat in its wake, the moon illuminating the glade where the gathering was held, and the darker corners cast in the glow of lanterns. The sounds of music and frivolity brought back memories to the wife, like in the mundane moments when you suddenly recall a dream from the night before, a memory that you had assumed was lost forever. For one night, she was wholly transported.

The bard had looked at her like no one had looked at her in a long time, and when he performed her a new song on his lute that was just for her, it was an altogether new kind of magic. It wasn't like the magic of the witches or the dark magic the husband abused; it was raw and it was beautiful, and perhaps she ought not to have kissed him, but it's possible that two feelings can inhabit a single moment, and you can feel ecstasy and the depths of shame all at once. You have to understand though, that the wife didn't do anything to hurt anyone — for the first time in a long time, she did something for no one other than herself. And really, what's wrong with that?

I have no idea how the rest of the plates got broken. The wall though, that had always been a bit shoddy, you just had to push against it the wrong way with your knuckles; it definitely *wasn't* a punch, not exactly.

The dark magic was too strong. After that night, the wife knew she should leave, go stay with one of the witches or run off with the bard, but the magic made her stay. She woke up early the next morning, swept the broken bits that had slipped beneath the oven, and went to pick up their son. She went to the chicken coop on the way back to get fresh eggs, and when she returned the curtains were still closed tight, and she and the little boy had to be very quiet, so as not to wake the husband.

"Why is Daddy still sleeping?" the little boy asked, as she gently worked the spatula beneath the bubbling membrane of the eggs on the stovetop. She allowed herself to focus on the eggs longer than necessary, to think for an extra moment.

"He had a very busy day yesterday," she replied finally, not untruthfully.

When the husband finally awoke, she placed the cooked breakfast in front of him (served on the skillet, since that was the only thing left), and the little boy sat on his lap, regaling him with the stories of his adventures from the day before, and the husband sat as a rapt audience member. The wife watched him carefully, silently, and wondered whether anyone would ever treat her son so kindly as the husband.

After breakfast, the husband offered to take the boy to town, to give the wife a reprieve so that she could clean the house. She decided not to venture to the glade by the brook, even though they were gone for hours. When the husband and the boy returned, she was surprised to see the boy bouncing along well ahead of his father, while the husband led a small horse by a lead.

"Mom! Mom!" cried the little boy, practically bursting out of his skin. "Guess what we've got!"

"Now remember," the husband said, when he reached the house with the mare, "Daddy said it's okay for you to have this horse, but it all depends on if Mommy is fine with it. After all, Daddy works during the day, so Mommy would have to be the one to stay home and look after it. What do you think, Mommy?"

The husband looked at her with a hint of a smile. Her son looked at her, holding his breath. She looked straight ahead and tried to remember a dream she'd once had about a party in a clearing in the sweet heat of the summer, but found that all traces of it were erased from her memory.

"Of course," she told her son, her eyes not straying from the husband.

The dark magic was very strong indeed. That night, when the husband was asleep, she crept out to where the old encyclopedias were on the bookshelf, and tried to find out how long horses live for. Her candle burned out before she found the answer, and she returned to bed unsatisfied.

Ever since he was a young man, the husband had been told that his job was to provide. It was a difficult burden to carry at times, but it was one that he did without complaint, day in, day out. In much the same way as he hauled himself onto the roof at the first sign of a leak, so too did he patch the first cracks of the witches' incantations on their idyllic little family. He had caught a faraway look in the wife's eyes and perceived her gaze going beyond him and beyond the forest. His job was to provide for his family, even if one of the foundations of that family was conspiring to cause it to crumble.

The route that they'd taken to the town that morning was a little out of the way, running by the farmlands. He couldn't remember how they had started talking about horses, if he had brought it up or if the little boy had — not that it mattered, what mattered was the absolute look of delight on the small face when he had the chance to brush the mane. And once presented with the option of being able to take her home, well, that had sealed the deal. And so he continued to provide, not just a new family pet, but a patch on a leak that had the potential to drown them all.

Watching the little boy run up ahead on the lane, so excited and carefree, he couldn't help but allow himself a rare moment of satisfaction at what a good father he was.

A long time is how long horses live, the wife found out a few days later.

The little boy had been eager to help, initially, but the dirty and mundane tasks soon bored him. The windows of time for sneaking out to see the witches disappeared, as she was either too tired or, more likely than not, occupied with the household tasks that piled up while she was out mucking the stalls or grooming the horse.

A year passed, then two, and the vitality the witches had once brought to her became a dull memory, not unlike the bruises that were occasionally concealed beneath her shawls and cardigans. When the idea came to her, it was not precipitated by any outburst or particularly late night in the village. It came to her unexpectedly while out at the market, baskets draped over the horse's broad shoulders to carry groceries back to their cottage. The little boy had decided to come that day, and was seated on the mare's back

It was a plain, simple, and perfect idea. "Why are we going this way?" the little boy asked, when they came to the crossroads and turned left instead of right, on the road away from the cottage.

She didn't answer, and instead hiked up her skirt and ambled onto the horse's back behind the little boy. The mare wasn't used to that much weight and wouldn't be able to carry them forever, but it didn't need to — with a nudge, it went off at a brisk gallop down the road towards the mountain pass. By twilight, they had gone much farther than they ever would have on foot, even allowing for extended breaks. By the third day, they were farther than either of them had ever been before. The forest lay far behind them, with only the open sky and fresh breeze ahead.

Once the ferry pulled out, that was when I remember a change coming over Mom, like she'd been holding her breath for hours and had finally allowed herself to exhale once the shoreline started to slip away. I don't know if she had a destination in mind when we docked in North Sydney, just that every passing town placed one more obstacle, one more blip on a map, between us and what we left behind.

It was summer, and she settled on a small town in New Brunswick, renting a small apartment by the week. It wasn't long before she got a job in Fredericton, about twenty minutes away, and found a babysitter in our complex. I enrolled in school in September.

By Christmastime, I was starting to ask about Dad in earnest. She found ways to waylay me, but by the spring, when I turned eight, she gave me his phone number. I'd like to think that I'd just become too annoying and she finally gave in, but I have a sinking feeling in the pit of my stomach, a gross feeling that still comes back to me every so often, that I'd said some pretty cruel things, and I broke something in her that had been weakened long ago.

That summer, I was allowed to come back to Newfoundland for two weeks. By then, there had been a yearlong break in the bedtime stories, and I'd hoped that in the passing of time, Dad would have thought I'd outgrown them. Instead, he picked up right where he left off the very first night I was back in my old bed, and when he found out Mom was dating someone new, he introduced a new character (a creature from the swamplands with a Miramichi accent) in a tale that became downright sinister. The only thing worse was when Mom found out, and kept the twisting narrative going once I was back with her. It was around then that the husband in the story started bleeding acid.

Here's the thing: I always knew the stories they were telling me were just stories. Even as a child, I knew that they were a simplified version of something, that the real world was more nuanced than the world of pretend. In a bedtime story, there always had to be a villain — in my life, it wasn't always as black and white as that. But just as I could plainly see that fact, I could also tell that they believed them. Even when the family as I knew it was falling apart, I never saw the full extent of the darkness, and after the separation, I found the back and forth from place to place just part of a grand adventure. But those bedtime stories, they somehow always gave me nightmares.

I was fifteen, just back from spending Christmas with Dad and his new wife. Mom had delayed everything—the tree decorating, the turkey, the gifts—until I came back, and we were surrounded by lights and wrapping paper on December 28. The dog that Dad and I had picked out that afternoon as a last-ditch effort to tie her to that place was asleep by the propane fireplace. It was then that I finally asked her.

"You remember those stories you and Dad used to tell me, about the family in the woods?"

She smiled a sad smile and nodded. "I haven't thought about those in a while. That was a very hard time for us all. What about them?"

By then, it had been a few years since either of them had brought me back to that dark fantasy world. "How did the story finally end?" I asked.

She didn't know, of course, that I'd asked Dad the exact same thing three days earlier, and I definitely didn't tell her that his reaction was almost exactly the same as hers. He was a character in her story, just like she was one in his, and even though things were much better between them by that point, neither wanted the other to be a sympathetic character just the same.

She stopped, thought, and then answered honestly: "I don't know, sweetheart. I don't know if it ever really ends, it just sort of . . . pauses. Lucky for us, you always fell asleep before the ending."

It had been more or less exactly what I was expecting, but I couldn't help but be profoundly disappointed. I knew then why the stories had always upset me so much, and the realization filled me with something that I recognized then as my first real adult sadness. Each one of us had come through what happened wounded and scarred, and even though life continued (which I knew was the real blessing for everyone involved), neither of them were able to allow that final release of that single unhappy kernel, lodged within themselves so deep as to be almost imperceptible.

For me though, I was old enough by then to tell myself stories to put myself to sleep, and to choose my own ending, that elusive conclusion I'd been chasing for the better part of my childhood. That night, with the glow of the neighbours' Christmas lights slipping in through the blinds, I whispered to myself: "Somehow, as the little family in the woods grew further apart, they all lived happily ever after. The end."

If I had any nightmares that evening, they were forgotten in the morning.

Corinne Lewandowski

Corinne is an award-winning poet from Halifax, Nova Scotia whose previous credits include poetry published in Loose Connections and poetry that won the Joyce Marshall Hsia Memorial Poetry Prize.

She currently lives in Lower Sackville with her wife and two cats.

Her first published prose story was 'Family Business' in *Dystopia from the Rock*, followed by 'The Final Invasion' in *Pulp Science-Fiction from the Rock* and 'Only Deities Need Apply' in *Mythology from the Rock*.

She brings with her her story 'The Beat of a Different Drone.'

The Beat of a Different Drone

Bleat! Bleat! Bleat!

"Whaaaat?" The flat surface of the cot became a steep slope, and Cinz stopped a faceplant on the concrete floor. "I was sleeping!"

A handspan away from her face, the blur of sapphire and pink sparkles of light bounced off the glittered face of her stepsister, Mitzy.

"Wake up, lazy!" She tapped her leg with a kick.

"My shift starts in seven hours!"

Cinz pushed up off the floor. Lizzy, the eldest stepsister, reached down and yanked Cinz's wrist, making her fall. She slapped on a digital work tracker and started its timer.

Cinz was yanked up to standing by Lizzy. "Not anymore. You're doing our cleaning shifts too." Lizzy joined Mitzy by the door of the utility room.

"Where're you going?" Cinz tested her shoulder and wrists to check for damage.

Mitzy held up her tablet. Strobing rainbow colours burst out, sparkling and streaking off the room and containers of supplies. Techno music shattered off the small space. Cinz's new cluster headache throbbed in time to the sound.

"Mumsy is getting us new outfits to make the right impression! We're VIP Gold Bandguests to DJ ESZ's Spectacular tomorrow! This mix has been number one for over a year."

Duh! You've played it Every. Single. Day. More sparkles than substance.

Cinz pulled on her utilitarian work coveralls over boxers and a tank.

Stepmother "Mumsy" Bitsy convinced them to put everything in her Mum's name to let insurance cover it, so they signed the docs. The probate revealed the ruse. Bitsy had never bought them anything but loaded the business' debt. Penniless and responsible for debt to Bitsy, Cinz couldn't get a free or paid lawyer to sort it. She owed six figures.

"Yeah, yeah. Have fun." She dragged her customer service smile into her words. Slighting her stepfamily might cause them to fine her for insubordination.

"Do the vents, drains, and boardrooms before your shift or the contract goes south for Mumsy!"

Crap! They'd done nothing. Fifteen minutes to bike there and she had ten. She slammed into her Mum's worn-out Docs and tore at the digital work tracker to get it off. Cinz didn't need a counter to mark down to the wrong kind of screwed.

It was locked on.

"We'll pick it up before the client's morning shift starts. After all, we're the pretty front of the business."

At the door, the sisters sing-songed in unison: "Better

go or more debt you'll owe!"

Every. Flippin'. Day.

Cinz jumped on her bike, pumping hard on the pedals.

Ding. Dong.

"We're closed! You don't look dead asleep."

Lela Bianco, proprietor of Lela's Clean and Fix it shop, didn't look up. Her reading glasses perched on her broad Filipino nose and the light of her tablet cast an orange tint on her dark brown skin.

"You never close for me!"

Cinz chuckled. She'd seen her working, but not like this. World-famous Drag King Lela Bianco had her Freddie Mercury wig and moustache in place. She wore the white pants striped with red, a white muscle shirt and yellow leather jacket. The juxtaposition in front of the garment conveyer need documenting. Cinz raised her tablet.

"No pics in the shop! I'm leaving for my show. What's up?" Lela Bianco hoisted a garment bag over her shoulder, the bottom barely clearing the floor.

"The sisters are too busy shopping to work. Gotta test my tweaks on the cleaning drones and hope they get me across the finish line."

Lela tossed the door fob to Cinz and a big grin lit up her face. "You've never failed before despite them. You got this." She snapped her fingers. "Lock up, engage security, and come over for breakfast to drop off the fob."

Ding. Dong. She left.

Cinz checked her locked stash at the shop to ensure

she had everything, then tossed her duffle on her back. She stood and pumped hard on the pedals of her ole reliable, no speed bike.

Lela Bianco's my lucky charm. Little miracles. Green lights on the all the bike lanes.

"I'm stoked for the stats," Rupert inspected the last drone against the manifest from Chief of Security Salazar.

Cinz checked in with her biometrics. "Come up on break and check the action." Staff were off-site working for preparing the DJ ESZ Spectacular and left the building empty.

"Everything is cuter with googly eyes! They need eyes." Rupert took selfies with the bot.

"No posting 'till I okay it!"

"Awwww," echoed from Rupert through the closed elevator doors.

Cinz made quick work of lining up her drones to charge. The sun pouring through the large boardroom windows was more than enough to top up their charges.

She cleaned as she assessed the chaos left behind by her family. Repurpose bins were overflowing, and tables were dirty. No staff had ever left glitter and lip prints on mirrors. The berry scent of Mitzy's trail clogged her nose.

What can I offer to any deities listening to have some peace from these two?

Caught up on the excess crap, Cinz checked on the drones. The Ducters had charged and self-deployed. She opened her program to show trails of six green lights.

Two were bellowing, starting their third floor. One of the Drainers needed the oxygen cleaning cartridge reseated.

"What's this about?"

An executive walked in. Sunset gleamed off their hairless head and face. The crisp power suit and shirt shimmered and pulsed in the hues of Ultimate Grey. Their ascot fluttered as if in a breeze. Smart glasses with moving workflows.

More credits than sense.

Cinz froze, holding the oxygen cartridge. "The enviro cleaning drones I designed."

"This smells great! No, not you. Hold!" Suits spoke at the smart glasses.

"Oh." She glanced at the time and reset the cartridge. "Thanks. We aim to please. Clean on time or we do it again!" The slogan made Cinz twitch.

"No, you *aim* to please. The regular day shifters are the laziest and are not meeting our standards." Suits' eyes focused elsewhere. "Hold on the email. Found a solution."

"How's this work?" Suits pointed to the drone.

Cinz prattled off the list. "Solar charged in twenty. Ozone Oxygen treatment to neutralize bacteria. Options for purifying water, video inspections, or custom coding. The program is synched to Rupert's security schematics."

Suits narrowed their eyes.

"Chief of Security Salazar authorized everything. You have sole access to data, audio, and video. The drones reference the data to clean effectively and not get lost."

"Hmmm." Suits waved Cinz over. She showed them her tablet. Green lines traced through the building showing routes. Remaining resources and issues were noted.

"Twenty hours to charge?"

"Umm." Cinz fumbled. She wasn't used to presenting. "Minutes."

"Turf the plan."

"I am sorry we didn't fulfill the contract. I'll just retrieve . . ." Cinz started packing.

Suits laughed. Animatronics were better coded to laugh naturally. They held up a hand to stop Cinz. "Bring up contract C-4920 for addendums. Back in five.

"Sorry, I didn't mean you. The company breeched the contract. These great critters you designed need to be in rotation."

"I'll tell the owner."

A paper thin smile crept up on Suits' face, humanity merging with the slick tech image. Eyes darted across their smart glasses. "I've messaged the owner you saved the contract."

Cinz's face went neutral. Rocks formed in her stomach.

"I advised the owner to demote the two-day staff. The contract will be amended to promote you to shift leader and implement the drones."

The rocks tornado-ed her guts. The air felt like it squeezed out of her body.

"To celebrate your success, take this."

Suits handed her a glittering wrist band with a hologram of ESZ rippling around it.

"VIP Onyx Band access to the DJ ESZ Spectacular tomorrow."

Cinz wondering if she could puke bounders.

"Umm. Really. S'okay. Not permitted to accept client

gifts. Not big on the music and crowds."

Suits choked out a laugh, then leaned in. "Not my idea of fun either."

Inhaling, Cinz relaxed a touch. *When they laugh, they look familiar.*

"We've several maintenance contracts up for renewal. We'd like you to apply. *Solo.* The owner will meet you at intermission to assess how you can fit with us. I'll get your schedule arranged. I know your innovation is inline with our principals.

"And you get to meet ESZ too." Suits smirked. They waved on the way out. "This place smells as fresh as day one!"

Lela Bianco screeched, and hot water sloshed out of the kettle as she poured.

Cinz's mug of tea almost flew out of her hand.

"Whaddayoumean You. Are. Not. Going?"

Cinz power scrolled through the messages. "My DM's are chock full of Evil One and Evil Two blaming me for everything from cleaning better than them to ruining their shopping mood." 'Mumsy' Bitsy piled on with, *Wait till I find the clause to let me fire and fine you.* "The timing sucks. I'll reschedule or something."

Lela shoved a bowl of fried rice in front of Cinz. She spooned over dried cured beef and slid on a fried egg to finish the Filipino tapsilog. "Eat this! You need *something* to get clarity. That," she pointed to the VIP Onyx band glittering on the table, "is opportunity."

Cinz broke the egg yoke over the rice and spooned

up a mound of breakfast. The garlic rice woke her. The luscious yoke and sweet cured beef made her palate sing. "Mmmmmm."

Lela chugged back a mango drink and flipped through the racks of clothing stuffed into her living room. *Scrape, scrape, scrape.* The hangers whooshed by. She had pieces of outfits stacking up before Cinz was done eating.

"One. You *don't* tell the CFO of Eco For Life you'll reschedule. *Or something.* Sweet Jesus." Lela Bianco added a pinstriped shirt and a purple sequined vest to the stack.

"Two. You don't no-show. One Onyx is issued per show. One. Word is, DJ ESZ is tight with Suits. Bitsy and her spawn don't want to improve."

Cinz drank a mango juice. No sense responding yet. Lela Bianco's spiels came in threes.

"Three! Yours truly is the show's intermission act!"

"Shut it!" Cinz leapt up and squished her in a hug. "How?"

Lela set a hand under chin and fluttered her eyes. "*Someone* knows a fancy DJ is a big fan. My people asked and I got the gig."

Cinz double-fist bumped the air. "Yes! More followers for you! Hunh? You've people?"

"Young thing, you're sweet and tech savvy, but duh. I've over 400mill. Think my drag king shows started yesterday? *As if* my singing and dry-cleaning biz are my only gigs. I have staff."

Cinz's face flushed with a different heat than breakfast and she switched the subject. "Who are you performing?"

Lela shoved open a space in the clothing rack to reveal

a collection of David Bowie outfits.

"Sweet! I love your Bowies! I'll be there for you and do the meeting."

"Had a feeling you'd go." Lela turned back to the clothing, blocking Cinz's view. Cinz needed extra help. The darker paths the stepfamily strode seeded more voids of self doubt in her. More light was needed.

A bright thin line of translucent purple particles wisped out from a shirt and touched Lela Bianco's finger.

Yes, thanks, that's perfect, she replied mentally. Then green Wisp reached out to suggest the pants.

The shoes for the outfit were pushed into Lela's hands by yellow Wisp.

Lela Bianco's powers of Faerie gawdparent worked in odd ways. Asking Wisps to do a thing was like blowing dandelion seeds. You never knew where or when it would root.

The Wisps hid back in her wardrobe racks. Peuple Wisp formed a finger and waved no to her. She agreed. Not the time to reveal anything. Cinz wasn't in *the* right place. She tucked away the Wisps' clothing choices.

Lela Bianco had more resources to call upon.

"Since yours truly is going . . ."Snapping her fingers, a fast temp DJ ESZ's track blasted out.

"Can't you play Bowie? Or eveeeen country. Anything else?" Cinz stuffed napkins in her ears.

"Try this out. I need to check your fit to make the best outfit." Lela pointed to Cinz's Docs on the boot mat. "Don't *think* for a nanosecond your mum's weathered Docs will work with any clothing for this meeting and the Spectacular."

Out of the corner of her eye, Lela caught the Docs huffing and wiggling at her. "Then get! You need rest!"

Metal screeched across concrete. Blinding light penetrated Cinz's eyelids. She flung an arm over her eyes to block the nightmare.

The nightmare materialized and breathed on her face.

"Get. The. Hell. Up."

Propping up, Cinz's saw she was in the hall. The stink of coffee, whiskey, and eggs shouted at her.

Long black tendrils of her stepmother Bitsy's hair extensions dragged past Cinz's face, the floral stink suffocating her.

"Ungrateful child! Know your place. You don't talk to clients."

Cinz swung her legs to floor and sat with her palms out. "The client spoke to me and declared the changes. Otherwise, they said the contract was breeched. Our client was grateful."

Bitsy grabbed the edge of the cot and dumped her backwards on the floor.

Mitzy and Lizzy snorted.

Great, a family affair!

"*My* client! You work for *me*. You don't cherry pick tasks and schedules. Or use your ugly looks to sway the client to your bidding. You don't speak for me or my company. *Ever*."

Cinz bound up. "Mum is dead and we are *still* a family. You *loved* each other!"

Bitsy shoved a tablet under Cinz's nose. The red glow of a six-digit number blinking. "Pay off your debt. Work for me or go to jail."

Cinz picked up her bedding and took it back to the utility room. "The client made the changes. I'll be on time for my midnight shift. I'm sleeping 'til then."

Mitzy and Lizzy blocked her way.

Lizzy wagged a finger. "Contractually, your shift starts at 12am and mandatory overtime will be our jobs today. Mumsy trumps the contract. The contract says so." They snorted at her.

"Come daughters, we're getting shoes for the DJ ESZ Spectacular Event."

Bitsy paused at the exit. "Finish their tasks two hours early. Breech of contracted schedule and targets will cost you two grand today. Time enough to design drones, time enough to clean."

Cinz's clenched the cot, her teeth were grinding and she was overheating.

Say *nothing*! Say *nothing*! Say *nothing*! *She doesn't know about the meeting.*

"Screw anything else or talk to the client and I double your debt."

Clang-Bang-Bang, the cot bounced.

"Five hundred for disrespecting my property. Oh." Bitsy looked back. "I never loved your mother. She was an employee. Just *like* you."

The wind dried Cinz's tears. Her heart gripped her mum's tales of love for Bitsy. Venomous Bitsy would not break her.

"Goddamn!"

Cinz clipped a bike-swallowing pothole and weaved to regain control. Crud splashed up adding marks to the white-rust-white patches on the frame.

Heaving for breath and calves on fire, she secured Ole Reliable in an Eco For Life's locker. She logged her retina scan and thumbprint. Exactly on time.

"You need an electric, Cinz." Rupert coordinated on-site security. The water he passed her was downed in one long swig.

"I got these calves pedaling." She headed to collect her drones.

"Yo! No need. Chief of Security Salazar let Cranky One and Uptight Two get them. Claimed maintenance."

Cinz's jaw clenched. She forced it to relax. "To maintain, you'd need to know how things work."

Rupert shrugged an apology.

Cinz turned back to him. "Not your worry," She swung her packsack around. "Good thing I finished Widget's upgrades. All knowing and seeing, it won't miss anything. Sign 'em in." She powered up Widget.

Rupert reviewed the specs. He inspected Widget's sensors. Multifaceted spheres covered the front and rear. A sensor winked at him and sent the image to Rupert's tablet. He moved away with a start.

"Googly eyes, I said. This is creeptacular. And not cute."

Between the bulbous new sensors, multiple legs and six rotors, Rupert rolling his chair further away.

"You watch zombie shows!"

"Humans are the real monsters."

Cinz popped Widget into the access vent shaft at the rear of the office and engaged the coding. "Widget starts at the top, then returns to you. You have the access codes to adjust video feeds." Cinz pointed at Rupert's screen. "Same as the others, but a titch faster and cleaner AV. I'm off to the races."

"Wow, Widget's already up." Rupert waved her off. "Private elevator is faster. Lightspeed! Go fast like your creepo-bot. Those stepsisters did diddly-do before they took the bots."

Cinz cursed in multiple languages in her head. *How did they convince Salazar to give them the drones?*

The gagging stench winner was in one of the public access bathrooms on the ground level. Her special prize was cleaning the lack of aim. For. Every. Substance.

Buzz! Buzz! Buzz!

Cinz's packsack vibration startled her. She missed cracking her head on the toilet tank by nearly eating her scrub pad.

Ewwww. She sanitized her face.

The vibrations stopped.

Muffled, her Diana Ross ringtone pelted: "I'm coming out / I want the world to know!"

"Decline call! Oi! Lela Bianco, I don't have time to breathe!"

Cinz finished the stall and rinsed her face. The bathroom door flung open.

"Time to breathe, time to speak! Decline my ass!" Lela

Bianco snorted. "I'm due in hair and makeup. Come now! I've your things!"

Cinz held up her pink rubber-gloved hand, while scrubbing the counter. "Can't! Wretches stole my drones. Bitsy is livid. Debt will rise faster than dough if I'm late."

Lela grabbed a pink cuff and whipped it off Cinz in a blink. "Check your tablet." Lela tossed the glove into the recyclers, washed up, and headed into the hall.

The Fifth Force of Nature that was Lela Bianco could only be mollified by compliance. Cinz needed her fortitude to make the deadline. Since her mum's death, Lela had been a true friend and never did a thing to Cinz's detriment.

Widget's tracker showed it was done her stepsisters' work. Cinz would celebrate when she had time.

Lela snapped her fingers as if in a Spanish dance. Trackers popped on Cinz's screen for every snap. The dozen new signals were doing work identical to Widget. She popped open the nearest vent to see Lela's drones.

Multiple compound eyes on a large fuzzy body glared back. A harry leg snapped the vent shut.

Cinz jumped back and landed on her ass.

Chittering echoed down the shaft.

Lela laughed and opened the rear entrance. "Your eyes are as big as those of my organic helpers."

The fresh air confirmed Cinz was awake. She felt her head. No bumps from the tank.

Wisps of green, purple and yellow shimmered like jewels of light, swirling around Lela Bianco. Cinz figured it was cool tech for the show, then the Wisps formed hands to wave hello.

"Against the regs, but you've got to be on time!"

"You never fail to surprise."

Ole Reliable was shiny with a bright white paint job. The frame was stronger and sported an electric motor. A garment bag and shoe bag were in a rear cart. The yellow Wisp weaved around the handlebars.

"What's this all about?" Cinz ran a finger along Ole Reliable, her oldest confident. The yellow Wisp twirled around her finger, then patted her hand.

"Go! We got it covered. This is not an event to miss. Change at the shop!" Lela mentally asked the Wisps to give Cinz space. "You're so not a horse and carriage kind o' woman.

"Still didn't answer." It felt good to sit on Ole Reliable.

"You didn't think you had a Fae-rie gawdparent, did you?" Lela gestured at herself. "Ta-Da! Isn't that what people say when there is magic?"

Cinz felt stress melt. *Mum said I'll be looked after.* She started the motor. It purred so hard; she thought kittens were going to jump out.

I can do this!

"The outfit is spectacular! Best with the shoes we picked!" Lela called out to Cinz as she built up speed down the alley.

"Spectacular is not being fired, jailed, or indentured for a million years."

Lela waved and the Wisps swirled around her.

"Yes, yes," she replied to their thoughts. "She will look great either way. And no, you're not telling her Wisps powered the motor. Yes, Yellow, you picked the shoes."

The VIP check-in at the DJ ESZ Spectacular was crowded.

Cinz couldn't see her entrance.

Tiers of standing room only platforms cascaded down towards the stage, holding tens of thousands. Access bands glowed, moving in waves with people dancing to the warm-up music. Throngs of every colour of the rainbow filled each area. VIP skyboxes boxes pulsed in metallics.

Cinz had trouble breathing. People. Noise. She lifted her mask, in case it was making it worse.

Lela Bianco wrote a note to wear the befitting outfit she picked to avoid extra attention. *No Docs* was underlined.

It was garish. The black mask flashed with neon purple trim. The silk shirt switched between lime green and neon purple. The black jacket's pinstripes changed colour in time with her shirt. The too-tight pants hugged her calves and punished her for choosing to wear her boxers.

Her Mum's weathered Docs grounded her and kept her from running out.

Business meeting, not a panic-sized-concert.

"I apologize. We were to meet you." The steward startled Cinz. She was taller and wider than the security staff, but radiated warmth as she held out an arm directing her.

Lowering her mask, Cinz stepped forward. The steward's security formed space around her. The bubble escorted her through an unmarked side door behind a wall of security.

Cinz thought she'd gone deaf. The hall was quiet.

"The VIP Onyx Lounge is upstairs." The steward directed Cinz to a large elevator, complete with beverages, an attendant, and a couch.

The steward went in with Cinz and faced the closed doors.

Cinz plunked on the couch and fully exhaled, then grimaced. *Don't wear boxers, she said. Could've told me why.*

Mitzy and Lizzy mingled with VIP Gold Band skybox friends, drinking gold sparkling cocktails and catching up in on the gossip.

Looking at the peons below, Lizzy choked on her sip.

Mitzy dabbed the wet spots off her sister's top.

"What is *she* doing *here*?" Lizzy pointed.

Mitzy looked at the VIP check-in. In a circle of security, they recognized Cinz before she pulled her mask down. She wore the top designer outfit with the dual-colour pulse shirt they were on the waiting list to buy. Cinz was swept away through an unmarked door.

"Rumour says that's the Onyx entrance," one of their new friends blurted.

Lizzy shoved her drink at Mitzy. She texted a flurry with both hands. *Ping!* A reply in her DM, she chugged her drink, then Mitzy's.

"Hey!"

"We'll be back in time! Meeting a resource to trim the deadweight in the family."

Lizzy grabbed Mitzy's arm, and they rushed out.

"All amenities are complimentary. The hospitality service interface is wired for requests by the table or voice. Or you can reach out to me. Ms. Ash will be here after the first set." The steward left.

The entry level had a full kitchen and tall chairs following a curved counter. The next level had seating and side tables. The best view level was filled with a massive deep, velvety violet couch, table, and two side chairs. Everything in the room was curved to face the enormous floor to ceiling window.

Cinz froze. The entire audience and stage filled the window. Vibrant outfits, most pulsing like hers, filling the space. At least she couldn't hear them.

"Dim lights, lowest settings."

"Dimmed. Windows may be adjusted. Do you wish to drop the two-way mirror?"

She caught a chair to prevent falling. She never expected the AI to ask her questions. "No. Lower inside opacity fifty percent." The concert goers were harder to see then.

Cinz settled on the couch in dark comfort. The couch was heated, and it curved around her sore spots.She kneaded the cushions like a cat. It hugged her like her mum's quilt of scraps. Her muscles relaxed.

She scrolled through the menu interface. The list had funky items. Haggis flavoured chips. Dulse chips. Only Red Smarties. Fries, dressing and gravy. Candy in any colour, type, or flavour.

A loud growl leapt out of Cinz. The tablet located her favorite nuts bars in the cupboard. Two bars were chased with fizzy berry water. Noises settled; she was confident the rumblings would be silent during the meeting.

The concert lights dimmed in the event hall and a gentle chime sounded.

Cinz allowed low volume in and increased her opacity and munched Red Smarties.

What do people see in all this?

The event lights went black, leaving a rainbow sea. The crowd went still.

A spotlight encompassed a stool and a table with beverages.

The sounds of footsteps moved across the stage.

DJ ESZ walked into the spotlight. Her long black hair tumbled over her shoulders and a short-sleeved V-neck tunic. The linen tunic stopped mid-thigh and flared over black pants that hugged her legs. She wore virtual controllers on both hands.

The lounge displays did a closer shot of DJ ESZ. Cinz could see hand-embroidered flowers following the neckline. Her outfit showcased her warm tawny skin.

"Thanks for coming. I appreciate all you do to make this possible." She waved to the crowd, who clapped politely.

"All of you make a difference." She looked to every section of fans and skyboxes, who clapped in turn.

Cameras switched between her face and the skyboxes.

The window filled with DJ ESZ's face looking at her. Cinz sucked in a breath. DJ ESZ's bright and violet eyes looked at *her* not *through* her. She gave Cinz a nod and smiled.

"Never think that you don't!"

The window reverted to the event space.

"Let's have fun!" DJ ESZ lifted her hands. The music raced up to a fast tempo and nature images projected everywhere. She conducted the music with her whole being. Swaying her hips and moving her head, she triggered sounds and images with intricate hand motions.

Cheers exploded with hoots, screeches and *I-love-yous* from every level. The vibrations of the bodies dancing thrummed low and deep through the lounge.

Cinz lowered the volume.

That was an entrance.

Oh, that's how bots will charge faster. Cinz smiled.
For here
Am I sitting in a tin can

Adjust tin can parameters. Wait. What? She frowned.

Far above the world
Planet Earth is blue
And there's nothing I can do

Cinz snorted awake.

Lela Bianco was belting out the last verses of Bowie's Space Oddity. She was suspended in a space capsule and leaning out its window singing.

DJ ESZ's music had an undercurrent that inspired Cinz's creativity. She fell asleep planning bot modifications.

Her Docs were tucked under the table. Her mask, tablet, and demo drone had been carefully moved to the far right of the table. Steam floated above the table, filling her nose with warmth and the smells of platters of Turkish food. The strangest moment was realizing she was under a blanket.

DJ ESZ was in a chair, leaning over her plate, shoving kebab, rice, and sauce in with a pita hand-to-mouth. She guzzled half a bottle of basil seed pomegranate juice.

"Sorry, I woke you. I power-eat at intermissions." Two more bites vanished.

Cinz sat up, pulling off the blanket. "My apologies. I didn't mean to fall asleep."

DJ ESZ's laugh was as warm as her skin tone. "That couch," she said, passing Cinz an empty plate, "is the knock-out queen. I never sit in it 'til after the show."

Between loading her plate with rice, baba ghanoush and falafels, Cinz stole glances at DJ ESZ.

The musician's hair was shorter than on stage. She had it in a short ponytail and wore casual black track pants and a long-sleeved shirt. She managed to eat two more kebabs.

Cinz set her plate down and turned to properly introduce herself. She glanced at the clock over the kitchen island. Lela Bianco's show was done in thirty minutes.

She creates great music, but where is that CEO?

Catching the glance, DJ ESZ cleaned her hands. She clasped Cinz' hand with both of hers.

"Pleased to meet you. I'm Morgan Ash, the owner of Eco for Life." She squeezed Cinz more firmly. "You didn't expect it to be me."

Cinz didn't know her jaw dropped until Morgan chuckled.

"Aspen is my CFO and may have mentioned you were in the dark."

The frown on Cinz's face caused Morgan to amend her explanation.

"Ah. We call them Suits too!"

How does she know about that nickname?

"They pestered me to be here, but I prefer these meetings be one-on-one."

Cinz looked at her plate and drank, wishing she'd wore the mask. Tiredness took charge and she giggled.

"I thought they were smirking!"

Morgan belly laughed, causing a chain-reaction in Cinz.

"The infamous smirk! Hmm. Aspen loves your drone tech."

"Thank you!"

Morgan blocked the sound from the stage. "Love her! Lela B and I go as far back as Suits. I met them at the same time."

The little plotter set me up!

Morgan put on binaural beats background music. It was calm and great for ideas. Cinz realized she had heard strains of it in ESZ's music.

"We all have different personas. My music is DJ ESZ. I'm many things. Sometimes just a woman letting the dappled light rock me asleep in a hammock. Connected to tree connected to earth.

"What you have…" Morgan leaned in close and reached past Cinz to touch the drone. "Is not tech. It's you."

"It leaves nothing behind," Cinz said after a moment of inhaling the vanilla and cherry scent left behind by Morgan and letting it swirl in her. Her favorite scents *and* flavours.

"Exactly! Don't look shocked. I talk to Rupert too. And Suits has been talking you up. We need you at Eco For Life."

"Yes, you do." Cinz felt confident. Energy flowed from being able to explore her passions again. "Look here." She touched Morgan's knee and scrolled the room menu items with her other hand.

"You're not all tech and music. EFL is sustainable for the planet and people."

Morgan was impressed with Cinz's deeper understanding her complexities.

"Thanks"

"But some of your vendors are reflecting only what you want them to say. May I?" Cinz patted her bot. It chirped awake and Morgan allowed it interface access.

"The vendor data from your hospitality." She handed the tablet to Morgan. "A shell company covering up plans to give its workers unfair contracts. Another doctoring ingredients. Both passed your vetting process."

Morgan speed read the data. "Not just a cleaning drone wiz. You're . . ." Morgan stopped, her cherry lips staying parted as she read more.

Cinz's tablet *ta-da-ed*. Avery delivered a lucrative contract from Eco for Life. The start date could be tomorrow. Multiple maintenance contracts with extra clauses to allow Cinz to submit new ventures in any scope. She looked at Morgan, then back to the tablet, then back at her again.

The signing bonus would free her of all debt owed Bitsy.

"Suits' timing is awful." Morgan's smile opened to show her teeth and she leaned in. "They beat me to the punch. Your proven innovation is what we need. No strings. One year deal with options to renew. Freedom to leave other *obligations*. I like to make sure we're a good fit."

"I . . . I don't know what . . ."

"Red Alert! Definitely not Yellow Alert! Midnight in five!" Her tablet overrode silent mode.

"Crap!" The tablet flew out of Morgan's hands.

Cinz leapt up, scooped up the drone and tablet, and dashed up the steps. Bitsy could unload more debt and trouble before Cinz could review this contract and hit send.

"You can stay!"

Cinz looked back. "I need to review. I'll message!"

She bolted out the stairwell exit, leaving Morgan holding Cinz's Docs and mask. "Where is she going?" Morgan asked the empty room.

Suits popped into the room through a server door, startling Morgan.

"Crap! You're going to kill me! Snoop!"

"She's brilliant! Go! Five minutes to your next set."

The room filled with klaxons bleating in threes. All screens were overridden with an emergency police alert. The house lights went up in the building and secure engaged lockdown.

Cinz's picture filled the screens.

Ding! Ding!

The private elevator opened and David Bowie entered, the tails of a Union Jack coat flying behind them.

"We have a problem," Suits said to Bowie.

"We need to talk, hun," Lela Bianco said simultaneously, removing her Bowie wig.

"Identify this person."

"It's me," Cinz squinted at the video and timestamp. The choppy image of her looked like she was connecting her drone into a server. "But it's not me."

Inspector Darwish sighed. "Be clearer."

Cinz turned her palms up while cuffed to the table. "Yes, the image looks like me. Yes, I worked in the building then. No, I was never in the server room. It's my image. It's not me."

"Ah, you recognize yourself in the server room!"

Cinz sighed back. "I see a fabrication that looks like me. A deepfake."

The inspector made notes.

"My presence is verified by biometrics and security personnel. Passes are coded for limited access."

Inspector Darwish showed Cinz the pass log. Date stamps had her going places she didn't. "Explain this!"

The door to the question room unexpectedly opened.

"Sorry, it showed unoccupied," said another inspector. Rupert stood behind the inspector, oblivious to Lela's yellow Wisps floating around him and the door.

"Rupert, Widget! Googly eyes!" Cindy hoped Rupert would get the message to turn in Widget's video logs.

Rupert nodded to her. As the door closed, Cinz heard Bitsy bellowing: "You'll lay these extra charges on her!"

Head dropping to her chest, Cinz cracked open her eyes. The chai tea she clutched was still stone cold. Inspector Darwish was uncuffing her.

"What?"

"You're free to go. The charges against you are dropped. On behalf of the Detachment, I apologise for the delay. We're grateful as your evidence assisted in catching the criminals. Your tablet and drone Widget will be released to you soon. Follow me."

Half-asleep, Cinz signed the release for her belongings. *Why is there a key card for a hotel room and note in here?* She smashed the button to turn off the still blinking outfit. Shuffling out, she wore the comfy sweats from the detachment.

"Hello." Suits, no, *Aspen* was standing on the front landing. Cinz could smell the hot chai tea she was offering her. "We've space booked at the hotel for as long as you need."

"Nope. Just need a good sleep on my cot. Done with chaos and neon."

Aspen matched her pace down the steps. "The police have deemed your home a crime scene. Your stepfamily is under investigation."

Unstoppable laughter forced Cinz to sit. "Bitsy always gets away with stuff."

Aspen tilted their head and had a double-creased frown. Then the infamous smirk appeared. "We're a large international organization. Getting caught selling proprietary data to international parties is the big time."

A bus with tinted windows pulled down the road by the side entrance. Aspen smiled as if they took credit for the timing of its arrival.

Bitsy, Mitzy, and Lizzy were hustled into the bus by a crew of policing staff. Cinz caught sight of a few CSIS jackets.

"My skin is going to chaff in this poly-cotton!" Mitzy wailed.

Lounging in a hemp housecoat as soft as Morgan's velvety couch, Cinz tossed aside her tablet. She spread cashew butter on her third vegan croissant. Three days in the luxuries of comfort, food, and not being scheduled to death was cathartic. New designs for tech were already flowing.

The view of sky and harbour were easy on the eyes and her head. Sunlight twinkled on the water. The mouth of the harbour at the horizon held the dark lines of a coming storm.

The only storms coming were for her ex-stepfamily.

Bitsy, Mitzy, and Lizzy had stacks of charges against them. Confirmation that they'd been watching her to use her couldn't yet dissipate the disgust worming in her gut and head. The croissants helped.

I was always the pawn. But not anymore.

The bathroom door opened.

"Are you going to steal all the bathrobes?" Cinz snickered, watching ferries pass each other.

Lela Bianco stuffed today's robes from housekeeping in a small bag with an impossible capacity. "Free fancy suite goodies! Get ready! Your meeting is in five. And give me that robe!"

Cinz made a short tease like she was stripping. She flashed open the robe to reveal she was fully clothed.

Ping! Ping!

"Get a going! Sui . . . Aspen texted that Morgan is coming up."

Morgan stood at the hotel door and it opened before she knocked.

"You can come in now."

Cinz's freckled cheeks were lit up with a wide grin. She headed back to a side chair.

Did she have a faux hawk with turquoise streaks on the back? Morgan hadn't notice that the night of the show. The streaks matched her linen top, which dropped a touch over black khaki pants.

"You look great! Clothes can make a person feel confident," Morgan said.

"Confidence helps me make better choices. Who am I kidding? Lela picked everything."

"The two must be in cahoots. Aspen hasn't let me pick a stage outfit since the first one. I wore jeans and a worn t-shirt."

Laughter broke the ice.

Cinz had snacks and beverages out. Morgan snapped up a rosewater basil seed drink and sat on the couch.

"Are you okay? That was a wild night."

Drumming her fingers on Widget, Cinz took a moment. "I lost a family, but it wasn't the one I thought I had, even when Mum was alive. Gonna take a bit to process. Mum's saying was any day your feet are on is a good one. Should've asked for her definition of good."

Cinz twirled her tablet in her hands and stared at Morgan. "This one-year contract is too generous. I'm unproven."

"The show night proved that untrue."

Cinz came over to sit by Morgan. "Why? Why not is no answer."

Straight to the crux and honest. That always drew Morgan in. "Maybe you haven't figured out where you're going. You're brilliant."

"Thanks." Cinz wiggled her tablet. "I have a plan."

The Cinz of before had been a glimmer. Today's confidence was enthralling.

"DJ ESZ is embarking on a world tour in two days.

"There's something I . . ."

Cinz decided to take the lead. "Let me. I'm embarking on a massive contract. My best work needs to come from my best place. So, my focus for a year will be healing and work."

Cinz passed the tablet to Morgan.

"You'll sign?"

"My old employer taught me what I didn't want in my life. Please review my addendums to the contract."

Morgan scanned and signed the doc, passing it back. She chuckled about some of the changes. "Someone's been talking to Lela B."

"She's always looked after me." Cinz put aside the

contract.

"I hear Eco for Life tries to embody collaboration and healthy relationships," Morgan picked up Cinz's tablet from couch and wiggled it. "Toxic crud is not tolerated from the bottom to the top."

"Oh yes, I heard you have an in with her," Cinz played along.

"I heard even the owner could get the boot." Morgan headed to the door. "Take your time. The only expectation is to play and be creative, and innovation will flow."

"No demands of me?"

"Well," Morgan turned back from the opened hotel door. "There is one . . ."

Ah ha!

"The RD team wanted to know your favourite things. You have an open invitation to their regular weekend retreat."

"And start the grind in a few days . . ." Cinz gripped the edge of the door.

"Not at all, Cinz. Mostly they asked if you are interested in board games, kayak versus canoeing, vintage or modern video games. All or none of the above. You're free to choose *anything, anywhere.* Anyone would be lucky to have you on board."

Morgan fished a small tablet from her bag and passed it to Cinz. "The team made videos to share what they love and hate about the work and their mean ole boss. And the hobby survey is included."

Cinz accepted the tablet.

"Let me know when you let me know."

Cinz closed the door and leaned on the cool surface,

flipping through the company tablet. *Rock hounding on the beach is a choice. Bet I can make a drone to spot fire agates on the ground better. How about that, mum? I'd get a living and acceptance for being me.*

Smart glasses on the table, Aspen rubbed their eyes.

"Untangling that hot mess Bitsy created tapped me out. Thank gawds they were caught. Damage repair is 24/7."

A bowl of tapsilog was set down. Aspen inhaled the smell of garlic. Lela Bianco added a pitcher of mango juice.

"Eat! You hate it when it cools. The important work is done. Our wards are in the right place at the right time."

Who says magic doesn't need help?

"No, dears, you're growed and don't need help."

Wisps of all colours played and danced around Aspen, the food, and Lela Bianco. The Wisps danced around a pic on the wall of Lela and Aspen smiling.

She lifted Aspen's hand and planted a kiss.

Heather Reilly

Heather Reilly is the author of the Binding of the Almatraek medieval fantasy series, and has written and illustrated several books for children.

Reilly is the proud recipient of the Noble Artist's Author of the Month award for February 2015 for her short story that appeared in *Fantasy from the Rock*, 'In the Moonlight.'

Reilly currently teaches music in Newfoundland, where she lives with her husband and three beautiful children.

Snow White and the Seven D.W.A.R.F.S

The brash crackle of the intercom sounded sharply in Cecilia's ear, alerting her that Ocean Blue was about to feed her more information from the space station. The bubbly female voice gave her the specs of the ship they were approaching as Grey Cloud guided them into their final docking position at one of the three ports they could see on this side of the gigantic vessel.

"You were right, Snow White, it's a relatively new ship. It's called the *Astor*, and it appears to be a botanical vessel. Its distress signal has been sounding for an hour. It was lucky that you decided to do a run today."

"What about life signs?" Cecilia asked. Onboard, her code name was Snow White, and she was the acting leader for this expedition.

"It looks like the scanners are picking up hundreds of instances of life, however, nothing appears to be moving. Be careful."

"We will," Snow White answered. "Thanks."

She smiled. Hopefully they'd be in and out before anyone else even heard the signal. Seven others were with her as part of a privately owned company of Demilitarized

Weapon And Resource Finding Specialists, or D.W.A.R.F.S. for short. They scavenged the demilitarized zone between two warring planets, and sold any goods they found in the debris to the highest bidder. If her hunch was right about the *Astor*, they may find crops or viable seeds that their top client would pay handsomely for.

It was odd: the ship had either been hit by, or had driven into a sizeable asteroid, which should never have happened if someone had been at the helm. This was the most exhilarating and nerve-wracking part of finding a new ship. She couldn't wait to open it up and see what was inside. But none of them really knew what might lie in wait for them beyond the air lock.

A slew of yellow lights began to blink in the cockpit as a succession of huge metallic clacks and clangs sounded at the rear. The docking arms latched onto the other ship, and the yellow lights on the dash turned a steady glowing green. The heavy hum of the engines cycled down as Grey Cloud pronounced them docked.

As they donned their white extra vehicular space suits, concealing their pale blue skin almost completely, they were interrupted by the deep and familiar sound of snoring.

"Wake up, Black Sheep, it's time to go!" she ordered.

"If you guys want to go on, I'd be happy to stay with the sleepyhead until I can get him up!" the most jovial member of her crew offered.

"Thanks, Purple Dragonfly. Send him along once he's conscious."

The man nodded and smiled amicably. She turned her back on him and the small group that was already prepared entered the air lock to disembark. What they were met with on the other ship nearly took Snow White's breath away.

All systems on the other ship were still functioning. The other airlock still had oxygen, heat, and lights, which they had not expected. The asteroid the *Astor* had collided with must have damaged the external engines without breaching the hull. That was amazingly lucky; perhaps all of the cargo would be undamaged and none would have been lost to the black endless void outside.

Snow White's inner-ears grew painful and popped with the change in the other airlock. She began to feel sweat prickle on her brow. Whatever crew they found would be from another planet, one where the air pressure and temperature in the atmosphere was naturally higher. This put her on edge. There was no telling if the race they found would be hostile or not. If they found anyone alive, they would of course try to help them. It wasn't a good sign that no one waited to meet them on the other side of the airlock door, either armed or not.

"Grey Cloud, hit the door release."

"Oh sure, drive the ship, Grey Cloud; hit the door release, Grey Cloud," he grumbled. "Why do I have to do everything? Is everyone else here incompetent?" he groused.

Snow White sighed. He was always in a bad mood. If he wasn't such a skilled pilot, she might consider letting him go. "If you're going to be grumpy about it, then I'm sure that our very capable Pink Blush can handle it."

"Aw, shucks," Pink Blush said bashfully.

"Go on," she encouraged. The man needed self-confidence, but she had no time to coddle him. She was getting impatient. The longer they waited, the closer another ship could be getting, and that distress signal would continue to sound until they could shut it down. "Hit the button."

Pink Blush lightly punched the large red glowing square with the back of his knuckles, and the door slid open. Snow White was almost overcome by all the green inside the *Astor*. The planet that her race came from was mostly covered in rock and water. The tiny clearing they were stepping into, however, seemed like a grove in the middle of a forest. They had studied other habitats, but knowledge from books couldn't hold a candle to actually experiencing what it was like. The white, brown, and burgundy trunks of the trees rose up all around them and were topped with leaves of every size and shape. Surrounding the grove, low-to-the-ground ferns and taller bushes sprouted from a layer of earth that seemed to have replaced the floor. She wondered how far down it went.

Snow White checked a computerized gauge on the spacesuit's sleeve to get a reading on the ship's atmosphere. It was rich with oxygen! It would make them a little light-headed perhaps, but it was still safe to breathe. She opened the latch on her helmet and pulled it off. Immediately her nose was met with the rich earthy smells of the soil. The air tasted impossibly clean on her tongue as she pulled in a breath to tell the others that it was alright. Yellow Ragweed pulled his off and tentatively sniffed at the air. He began to let out a succession of tiny sneezes that didn't want to stop. He quickly replaced his helmet, but it was too late. Silver Snake, their team's medic, took a look at him through the thick glass. Yellow Ragweed's eyes looked irritated and though the sneezes tapered off, he now sounded completely stuffed up.

"Snow White, I suggest we let him go back. It seems to be an allergic reaction. He can take one of the anti-allergen tablets in the sick bay." He looked to their leader and she nodded her consent.

"Thanks, doc," Yellow Ragweed said miserably as he turned to go.

"Now we have to find the helm and turn off that signal. I'll bet that's where we'll find the crew. I think we should prepare for the worst."

As she spoke to her team, Purple Dragonfly and the still-yawning Black Sheep caught up to them.

"We left Yellow Ragweed with the ship," Purple Dragonfly explained.

"Good," Snow White agreed.

They began to venture through the woodlands, and from somewhere much deeper in the ship, Snow White could hear a faint repetitive melodic sound.

"Let's split up," she decided. "Silver Snake, you take Black Sheep, Green Grass, and Purple Dragonfly and shut down that distress signal. I'm going to take Pink Blush and Grey Cloud to find where that other noise is coming from."

Snow White followed the strange sound until the woods gave way to an orchard. The fragrance was cloying as the branches, heavily laden with some type of red food, drooped low to the ground. Curious, she grasped one of the fruits and picked it. It was hard and fit perfectly in her hand. When she bit into it, she noticed that it was white on the inside, and her mouth flooded with a sweet juice as she chewed. It was glorious! She might have to keep some of the seeds from this for herself. The sound they had been following cut off for a moment and restarted, this time with a different tune. It seemed to be coming from the other side of the orchard where there appeared to be a wall of the ship and a large rectangular box.

Then the crackle of Snow White's com sounded again.

"Another ship is approaching. Have you found anything?" Ocean Blue sounded anxious.

"Maybe, give me a second."

The group raced across the orchard toward the mechanical box. The closer they got, the more it looked like a glass coffin. Tubes ran from the wall into it where controls monitored something's vital signs. Snow White peered inside and was instantly taken with the man that lay within. He was incredibly handsome, and looked exotic with pale pink skin. The music appeared to be coming from inside. She caught the phrase "Take me with you". *That's a brilliant idea,* she thought.

Metallic clanks echoed around them. Another ship was docking close by. Snow White hurriedly spoke into her com.

"We've found someone. He's alive, but in cryostasis. Ocean Blue, there's nobody like him… anywhere at all. He's pink!"

"You'd better get him onboard as fast as you can. Our data shows that the other spacecraft is the *Mirror*."

Snow White swore under her breath and spoke to her team. "We've got to get this guy up, Queenie's ship is here. Pop the hatch."

They exchanged nervous looks. Queenie had been caught smuggling live weapons into the demilitarized zone. Snow White and the D.W.A.R.F.S. had been the ones to apprehend her for the bounty, and Queenie had been banished as a result. Apparently, she had found her way back. All of their lives were in jeopardy.

Snow White nervously bit into the crisp red fruit again as the lid of the cryostasis chamber rose and the blast of music grew louder, declaring, "My name is Prince." They killed the music, removed his IV and sensors, and he began to come to.

"Prince, I'm Snow White. Your ship crashed, and we have to get you out of here, right now," she said around her bite of apple.

She reluctantly dropped the fruit and reached for his hands to help him up. He had begun to rise, when Green Grass shouted for her to watch out, and she felt something hard strike her in the back. The piece of apple she was chewing got knocked into her throat and she began to choke. The D.W.A.R.F.S. ran to subdue Queenie as Prince climbed from his box in an unsteady hurry, and spun Snow White around. Her bulging eyes saw Queenie with an armload of fruit that she was throwing at the D.W.A.R.F.S. Then the alien's chilly, strong arms were around her and he forcefully pulled his fist into her gut. The piece of apple sailed out her mouth and a rush of the oxygen-rich air filled her lungs. She had just enough time to regret taking off her helmet before she passed out.

Snow White's eyes fluttered open. She was in her own

sick bay, and she wasn't alone.

"Prince—"

"No, he's just a musician I love. My name is Florian. That woman that hit you with the apple is locked up, so you're safe now."

His hand was warm now as he tenderly brushed an ebony hair off her forehead.

"Where did you come from?" she asked.

"Earth. Once I reached a planet that could support my plant life and I, the ship was to wake me. But the course set didn't allow for an unexpected asteroid. You saved me, you know. I must find somewhere close by as soon as Green Grass is finished with the repairs to my ship. I was hoping you might know of somewhere, and that you might want to come with me."

She smiled and said, "I know just the place."

Teresita E. Dziadura

Teresita E. Dziadura has steadily been making her voice heard in the Newfoundland writing scene more and more over the last two years, making her presence known at NaNoWriMo writing events and seminars as a force to be reckoned with, bringing wit and insight to every conversation she's a part of.

She made her first mark in the world of published fiction with her short story 'Beyond No Man's Land' in *Chillers from the Rock*, a chilling tale that cemented her as one of the fresh new talents in the industry.

Dziadura describes herself as a sci-fi and horror nut, but is also a longtime fan of British comedy. She has studied Marine Biology and has four children with her husband of twenty-five years.

Her first novel, *Corporate Invasion* is available through Engen Books.

Scarlett Hood

The cafe was warm and filled with strong scents of coffee. The menu's header read, "Remember, a yawn is a silent scream for coffee". It was decorated for the season, with skeletons dangling from the lights, witches hiding in the potted plants, and smiling pumpkins and ghosts painted on the windows.

Scarlett was lost in her work, a steaming mug of chai tea latte in front of her. The scrape of a chair leg against the floor made her look up to see a man in his middle years helping himself to a seat opposite her with a flourish as he unbuttoned his sport jacket with a practiced flick of his wrist. She gave him a bemused smirk and said, "Yer welcome to join me."

He studied her for a moment before speaking. "Good afternoon, Ms. Hood."

She leaned back and raised an eyebrow. "Have we met, Mister…?"

"My name is inconsequential. I have a business proposition for you."

She tipped her head to the side as she studied him. The man oozed money, from the neatly coiffed silver flecked black hair, his deep blue eyes above the one-of-a-kind FG Taylors suit, and the polished Die Wichtelmänner shoes. Gold cufflinks and a matching tie pin, with the initial C inset in diamonds from "7D Mines and Goldsmiths."

A Charming? Can't be. Not here. Not for me, she thought. Her eyes flicked around her favourite haunt and noticed at least five patrons who stood out with their dark suits and sunglasses and conspicuous bulges around their ribcages or hips. His entourage kept a respectable distance from their employer, but they were there, watching, vigilant.

She put a practiced smirk on her face. "Well then, Mr. Inconsequential, wha' ken I do for yeh?"

He smiled at her. "I have a family member who is missing."

"Mhmm." She inclined her head, conceding his point. The movement dislodged a chestnut curl that hung between her eyes. She stuffed it behind her ear before continuing, "G'on."

"I'd like for you to find them."

"What about The Guard?"

His already narrow lips virtually disappeared. "No." She raised an eyebrow in question. He cleared his throat. "That would mean a formal inquiry. Something I'd rather not happen."

"Interestin'." She leaned forward and steepled her fingers above her laptop. "I'll be needing a wee bit more info."

He leaned down to a briefcase by his chair, removed a manilla envelope, and slid it over the table to her. The movement drew attention to a signet ring, an embossed shield bearing a snowflake. Her mouth went dry; he wasn't A Charming, he was THE Charming. Descended from the Kings of Faraway. Snow White's great-grandson. She swallowed hard. Her clientele did not come from such circles.

She opened the envelope and pulled out its contents: four photos of a young woman who looked to be in her mid-teens, each from a different angle. Her long black hair was in a braid and the front had been dyed like a rainbow; she wore a pink sweater and black leggings, but it was her eyes that stood out, blue like the colour of the summer sky, lips as red as rubies. Scarlett glanced from the pictures to the man before her. The girl was definitely a Charming. She flicked through until she came to a page of printed messages from the social media site, FairyTales. A quick read-through made her stomach turn to ice. Beneath that was a contract that included a payment with more zeros than she'd seen in her whole life. She looked back up at the man who sat ever so calmly before her.

"Will you help?" She took in the tightness in the way he held himself, the small lines pulled taut around his mouth. The calmness was a practiced facade. This girl was important to him.

"Aye, Mr. Inconsequential, I'll take yer case."

Scarlett walked up the stairs to her cozy office-apartment in the lower end of town. The old red door with frosted glass greeted her with its bold gold and black writing of her logo of a hooded cloak: "Hood Investigations: You lose it, we'll find it." The "we" was her.

She opened the door and turned on the light in her

small office. A couple of bookcases on the left wall and a single desk facing the door with two mismatched chairs facing it for clients. Behind the desk were a set of floor-to-ceiling windows that looked out on the river, filling the room with unfiltered, early evening sun. She laid her laptop bag on the chair and opened a door on her right that led to her cozy apartment. The living room and kitchen were one room, separated by a two-person dining table cluttered with bills and books. The living room was to the left of the door and the kitchen was to the right. Several day's worths of dirty dishes filled the sink. The bedroom and bathroom were off the living room. It was compact but it suited her needs.

A meow greeted her, and she looked down at Rumpelstiltskin, her petite tuxedo kitty who trotted up, his name tag jingling from his studded leather collar. She'd found him on her first case, helping a young single mother find the identity of an extortionist who was threatening to steal her child.

"Hey, Rumple." She gave the cat a rub between ears that looked too big for its head, giving him a bat-like appearance. "You hungry?"

A silent meow answered her as the cat wove its way in between her legs. Scarlett laughed as she opened a can of tuna flavoured cat food, wrinkling her nose at the smell, and dropped it in the bowl with a wet plop. She threw a frozen dinner into the microwave for herself, and changed into a set of comfy pajamas while her food warmed. The microwave beeped as she poured a glass of red wine from a box. "Only the best vintage to go with a two-coin frozen dinner from Market's grocery where the food is cheap, and they don't ask questions. Just don't look too closely at the best before dates."

She sat on her sofa, putting the tumbler filled with wine and the veggie bowl on the coffee table. Rumple followed her and sat cleaning himself.

"Got a new case and if it works out, we will eat like Charmin's," she said to the cat, holding up a photo of the missing girl. "Calliope Charmin'. Granddaughter to *The* Charmin' and sole heir to the family fortune." She cycled through the photos as she spoke. "She's been missin' since Monday. Dat's four days ago. The odds of findin' her alive are poor." Rumple tipped his head to one side and chirped. "Aye. Ye think they'd have called The Guard when she disappeared, but old Grandpappy Charmin' doesn't want the attention." Scarlett made a disgusted noise which the cat echoed. "'Magine puttin' public opinion afore yer own granddaughter's life?" Scarlett poked the photos back into the envelope and picked up the transcript. "As ye might 'ave guessed, there are complications." She held up the pages and let Rumple look them over.

"Pixie Dust?" Rumple looked up at Scarlett who only nodded. "It's bad stuff, Red."

"I know." She leaned down and gave the cat a kiss on the top of the head. "Think ye can help?"

Rumple stood and walked over to where Scarlett had the papers laid out. He studied them, moving some with his paw for a better look. After a while, he purred and looked up, put his delicate white paws on her chest, and gave her a head bump before disappearing out the window and down the fire escape. His voice carried over his shoulder. "I'll see what I can do."

Scarlett made her way to the small village of Gruselige Stadt, which sat on the edge of the Forbidden Forest. A perpetually dark and fetid wood filled with pitfalls and quagmires. It crawled with trolls, goblins, and witches. None of which any sensible person would want as a neighbour.

She'd been hired by Frau Naschkatze and she'd met with them just before entering into the hellscape.

"Guten Morgen." Frau Naschkatze was a tall woman with long fair hair she had tied up in a crown braid upon her head. Two small children peeked from behind her skirts. "These are mien kinder; Hansel, Gretel, say hello."

"Hello," they said in unison before disappearing behind their mother once again.

"You said your mother…"

"Ah, yes, mien mudder. She went into the forest two days ago, collecting mushrooms, and never came out."

"I'll do everythin' I can," Scarlett promised.

Scarlett was no stranger to forests. She'd grown up trailing after her grandfather, a woodsman, and thanks to him she could track almost anything. She found the old woman's basket, half-filled with mushrooms not far inside the forests edge. She looked around and saw the remains of several half-eaten fungi. She picked them up. "Oh no. Psilocybe cubensis. Or as the woods hags call them, magical mushrooms." She looked around and found a trail leading deeper into the forest. "Oh Nan, what 'ave you done?"

Scarlett woke to Rumple patting her face with a damp

paw. "You were screaming in your sleep. Again," he said as he moved to the bottom of the bed and began to lick his paw to dry himself.

She wiped the sweat from her face. "Washtimes'it?" She grabbed her phone and the bright digital display read four-seventeen am. It took Scarlett a few minutes to gain her equilibrium.

"That dream again?" Rumple asked.

"Doesn't matter." Rumple snuffed but let it go. "Did you find out anything?"

He lowered the paw he'd been licking. "That Charming kid?"

"Yeah?" Scarlett leaned forward.

"She's not the only one."

Scarlett swung her legs out over the edge of the bed and stood up, all chance of sleep gone. "Tell me everything."

Rumple had heard from the alley cats that Calliope wasn't the only kid to go missing. Seven of the local pets had their people gone missing. Some were rich, others poor, others homeless.

"All they know is that their people were meeting someone and then they never came home." His ears were laid back as he spoke and his whisker twitched. "It can't be a coincidence."

"I don't believe in coincidence, Rumple."

Scarlett spent the day reaching out using good old gumshoe techniques. Reaching out to her contacts in the press, family and friends of the missing, and her Guard contacts, only to be told that, "We don't know anything;" or, "while they appreciated her interest, they could not discuss any ongoing investigations." The harder she leaned, the harder they clammed up.

"Neptune's bloody shells!" She slapped the red hang-up icon on her phone and threw it down on the sofa next to her.

Rumple stretched and looked up at her. "No luck?"

"Stonewalled. At every turn. The Guard won't talk tah me. Her friends won't talk tah me. Even my contact at the Town Crier won't talk tah me. Hell, her own Grandfather is tighter than a mermaid's pet clam."

"What will you do?"

"No clue." A tapping at the window made her look up to see a pair of black shiny eyes peering in at her. "Lokes?" She opened the window enough to allow the raven in.

He made a deep gronk and tapped her hand with his beak. "'ave ye 'eard?"

"What?"

"Guards found a body."

"Where?" She was already pulling on her hoodie.

"Down by the bay, near where the watermelons grow."

"Thanks!" She tossed Lokes a biscuit and ran out the door.

The gathered crowd made it easy to find. Lokes had been right: the whole dock area below the watermelon farms had been secured and was crawling with Guards and Inspectors. Scarlett slipped between people until she made it to the area the Guards had cordoned off. She saw one of her contacts, Corporal Dav, standing nearby and she squeezed passed some gawkers to get to him.

"You can't be here," he said from the corner of his mouth.

"C'mon Dav. I just needs a peek."

"I can't."

"Just a little one?" She batted her green eyes at him. "Puhleeze. I'd be ever so grateful."

"By my fairy godmother." He rolled his eyes. "You're going to get me fired." He lifted the rope that had been used to keep the gawkers back. "Fine. Five minutes" She slipped under, and he put his hand on her arm, pulling her back. "It's bad."

She lifted a brow, and his face went tight. "Bad?"

He gave a quick bob of his head. "Bad. Inspector Brier-Rose turned green and gagged."

"She's hard as stone."

"Not this time." He let go of her arm. "Don't say I didn't warn you."

She slipped around the warehouses and inched her way closer to the wharf. Peeking from around a small boathouse, she saw the deep blue of the Inspectors' uniforms with their backs turned to her surrounding a prone form. Water lapped against the dock, hiding whatever they were saying. Scarlet needed to see what they saw. She pulled herself up onto the roof of the boathouse. Lying flat she pulled herself to the peak and peered over the top. She gasped and slapped a hand over her mouth to stifle the cry that tried to escape, nearly sliding off the tin roof in the process. Dav had been right. A halo of long blonde curls encircled the girl's head. It was the only way Scarlett could confirm the victim hadn't been Calliope. She dropped to the ground.

The sun had long since sunk behind the horizon when she returned to her apartment.

"You okay?" Rumple said, looking up from across a chessboard. Lokes made a deep croak and moved his queen piece. Three more moves and he'd have Rumple.

She shook her head. "Not even a little." She headed into the kitchen and took down a glass and filled the tumbler with the box wine. She took a long drink, turned back to the pair sitting on her small coffee table and filled them in on what had happened.

'What arrre you gunna do?" Lokes croaked.

"Right now? I'm gonna finish this drink and go to bed."

Scarlett stayed near the cottage, hiding in the woods. Something wasn't right here and she'd long since learned to trust her instincts. A stone dug into her ribs where she hid in the brush. She watched as an old woman did her chores, chopped wood, and fed her livestock. She took a bowl of something and went into the barn, leaving empty handed a few minutes later.

It felt like forever until the sun set and a large silver moon filled the glade in soft light and shadows. Scarlett stood from her hiding place and groaned. Everything ached from laying in the cold for so long. She slipped from the bushes and, sticking to the shadows, made her way towards the barn. She passed a midden filled with bones that looked far too human in the shadowy light. Some were old and faded, others were fresh and new. She gagged, trying not to think of the meat pies she'd eaten earlier that day.

Once she'd made her way to the old barn, she heard sobbing from inside. Cautiously she opened the door and slipped inside. The stench hit her like a wall. A mix of abattoir and sewer, it was too much for Scarlett after the midden heap and she doubled over, losing her lunch. Tears filled her eyes as she stood and wiped her mouth with her sleeve, taking in the scene before her.

"This isn't a barn, it's a prison." The straw lined stalls were separated by floor to ceiling bars of steel with locked gates at the front of each.

"Who's there?" a fear-filled voice called from the darkness.

"'I'm Scarlett. I'm looking for Ella Gruber?"

"Ella Gruber? That's me."

"Your daughter sent me."

A sob escaped from the shadows and the woman crawled into the half-light. She was bruised but otherwise healthy looking. An uneaten bowl of stew sat in the straw by her cage door.

"What happened?"

"She did." Ella pointed to the cottage which could be seen between the slats of the barn wall. "She calls herself, The Grandmother, but she's a monster."

"It'll be okay."

"No, it won't." Ella shook her head, dirty grey hair swinging back and forth. "I wasn't alone. There were three others. Kinders. I know their family."

Scarlett rubbed her face. A pit of ice was growing in her stomach.

"Braun, Scwarz Schwein, and their little sister, Weis." Her voice broke. "She took Braun the first day I was here and yesterday, Schwarz. This morning? Weis. She was only eight."

Scarlett woke in a cold sweat. Daylight filtered through her curtains, brightening her room which was filled with the smell of English breakfast tea and Belgian waffles.

"Monty? Rod? Lou? That you?" She mumbled, pouring herself a tea and inhaling the rich aroma.

"Monty and Lou Petter, at yer service m'am," Monty said in a very heavy Cockney accent.

She rubbed the sleep from her eyes and looked down to see mice of unusual size. The biggest at six inches long, was Monty, who was drying the last of her dishes. His brother, Lou, was plating waffles which he topped with whipped cream and berries and pushed over to her.

"Where's Rodney?"

"'ome."

"Is he okay?"

"'E's fine. Just sniffles is all. We figgered ye'd be fallin' apart by now. Wit us gone on 'olidays for a week." Monty waved his tiny paws around the space. "An' we wuz right."

"Sorry," she said in a sheepish tone. "I was working on a case." She picked up the plate and went to her laptop on her office desk.

"*Yer* a case," Monty said with a chuckle as they dropped to the floor and pulled out three-inch white canes to feel their way across the floor.

"What are yah workin' on?" Lou hopped up onto the corner of her desk and reached a paw out to steal a piece of her waffle. Waffle successfully purloined, he sat back on his haunches and began to nibble.

"Missing kid."

"Damn. Didn't think you did those no more," Monty said.

"Not after the Grandmo— Ooof." Lou was cut off by Monty's tail thwacking him on the head. He rubbed the spot with his paw, giving Monty a rude gesture that the other mouse couldn't see, but said no more.

"Yeah, well, this one's an exception."

Monty patted her hand with his paw. "If you needs us, just holler."

The two mice hopped down and, using their canes, made their way out the window and down the fire escape into the alley below.

Scarlett smiled after them before turning her focus onto her laptop. She spent the next few hours trying to locate the user Calliope had been talking to, BigBad1. Grandpa Charming had given her Calliope's login information and she had managed to figure out BigBad's internet service provider. Four hours on hold had led them to tell her they couldn't help, but she could send in a formal request for profile access if she had the right forms to submit. A twenty-second call to Grandpa Charming had resulted in a half dozen emails with all the paperwork she'd need. An email was sent then, and an automated reply appeared almost instantly letting her know how important her request was to them, and that they'd respond within the next 10-21 business days. "Neptune's shells," she said with a sigh and took a deep draught of her cold chai tea. "Almost a full day lost on this goose chase. Neptune only knows what's happened to her by now."

Rumple jumped up on her desk next to her. "He preys

on desperate girls." He looked at Scarlett from the corner of his eye. "You're desperate and a girl."

"Seriously?"

"Why not?" His shoulders twitched in what Scarlett called his cat shrug. "Can it fail any more epically than your last couple of leads?"

"You're an arse."

"Maybe," he murped and bumped his head against hers. "But I'm right."

Scarlett looked over the transcript again and clicked "New Account" on the FairyTale website. "RedHGrl, age sixteen." She uploaded a photo of herself at sixteen as her profile pic and typed one message. "Hey, new to the EForest area. Got finals coming up and need a little *assistance*. Anyone able to help?" She submitted it to all the same message boards Calliope had used and within minutes she received eight private messages, one offering tutoring services, one assorted drugs, and six random eggplant pictures. None were from BigBad1.

For hours she stared at the screen, vetting messages and blocking weirdos. "This was a waste of a day."

She leaned back in her chair, poured some bourbon into her now ice-cold tea, and took a drink. With a grimace, she laid it down and rubbed her eyes. She half-closed the laptop to keep its light out of her eyes, stood, stretched, and went to relieve her aching bladder. On her way back she grabbed some pot noodles from her cupboard and put them in the microwave. Sixty seconds later, it beeped, and she nearly missed the ping from her laptop. With a single movement, she removed the noodles, picked up a fork from her counter, wiped it clean on her jeans, and sat back down to see the message icon flashing. She tapped the icon with her finger, expanding the message screen. Her heart began to pound when she saw the message, "Hey, I think I can help." BigBad1.

Scarlett had to respond now that she was on reading. She glanced over Calliope's messages and decided to take a similar approach.

"I sure hope so. I'm screwed without it."

Almost instantly three dots floated in the bottom left corner, and she smiled.

"Whatcha need?"

"Whatcha offering?"

"You first."

"I need help with math."

"This isn't a tutoring service…"

"Oh. Will other things really help?"

"I wouldn't make money if it didn't."

"I don't usually do this...?"

"It's okay. I can walk you through it. But I need some assurances first. How do I know your not a Guard?" Followed by a popular SciFi meme with the words, "It's a trap!" on the bottom.

She let the dots float for a bit. Letting him think that she was writing and erasing message after message.

"I'm not a Guard. I go to Persophone High, down by the harbour."

"I need assurances."

"TheCharming1 told me about you."

"You're Charms friend?"

"Yeah. In real life too."

Fairy Tales from the Rock 155

"What's her favourite Dust?"

"Blue." It was the only one she'd ordered in transcriptions.

"That works. YOu want to forget or remember?"

"Remember?"

"Red it is."

"How much?"

"I've got 15 coin. My allowance." Her hands were sweating, and she took a deep drink of her cold tea and bourbon.

"For Charm's friend? I'll do bogo, so 10 g of Dust.'

"Thanks!"

"We can meet by the Peter Pan statue in BoPeep Park. Noon."

"That's pretty secluded."

"These transactions don't go down in public."

"Stranger danger…"

"Fine. How about behind Gingerbread Bakery after school on tomorrow?"

"Fine." Scarlett closed the app.

"You know it's a trap," Rumple said, stretching and wandering over.

"I know."

"Whatcha gonna do?"

She ran her fingers through her hair, pulling it out of its ponytail, which made itstick off in all directions.

"You could call *them*."

"No."

"It'd work."

"I know, but I'd 'av to beg."

"And we all know Re—" She shot him a glower. "I

mean *Scarlett* doesn't beg."

"You suck."

He patted her arm with a paw. "It's to save a kid."

"You really suck."

"But I'm right."

"Ugh!" She picked up her phone and scrolled through her contacts, coming to stop on M. Piper and a picture of what a mynah bird would look like if they were human and wore haute couture.

"Hey, Piper. Yeah, it's me, Scar—" She paused and sighed. "Yeah, it's Red. I know it's been a while—" She held the phone away and Rumple tapped the speaker with his paw and a shrill voice pierced the air. He hit it again, muffling the tirade, and flinched. "Sorry," he mouthed. "They are still *that* angry?"

"Seems like," she whispered back.

" I know. I know, Piper. I'm sorry. I deserve it all an' more." She hung her head and sighed. "I wouldn't have called if it wasn't important. I'm tracking a missing kid."

Scarlett began to nod. "Yeah, hang on, Rumple's here." She hit the speaker button again

"—and don't you ever do that again. If you do, we're through for good."

"Hi, Piper," Rumple said with a purr.

"Hi, fluffball."

Rumple's whiskers twitched in a cat smile. "You gonna help our girl out?"

"I shouldn't."

"You will." Rumple chuckled. "She needs your help. He's a predator."

"Oh for fu… fine, but only because you're trying to

catch a predator."

"I knew we could count on you." Rumple purred.

"Of course, Piper Tech is at your surface."

"Great," Scarlett interjected. "Gonna send yah some stuff. Can ye trace a user for me?" She clicked her keyboard.

"If he's on the interweb, I can find him."

"I owe you."

"You more than owe me. Once this is over…"

"Yeah, I know, we're gonna have long talk. Thanks."

"Got it." The sound of clicking could be heard over the phone. "Oh, this is going to be fun…" And then the line went dead.

"That was awful."

"I'm gonna get you outta here."

She looked around and grabbed a small hand spade that was nearby, hammering on the lock. It skimmed off, nearly stabbing her in the leg.

"Do you think you can do it?"

"No think, just do." She said, misquoting one of her favourite movies. "This won't work though."

"You should go before she hears you."

"I made a promise." Scarlett disappeared back outside, returning a few minutes later with the axe she'd seen Grandmother using earlier. She swung the butt of the axe down and heard a crack, but it was loud. She stopped, axe held in the air and when no one appeared, she struck the lock again and again. Finally it fell apart and the door swung open.

Ella's eyes filled as she stepped through the open door.

"Thank you."

They kept to the shadows, working towards the woods. A voice called from the open window: "Who's there? That you, Rolf?"

"No." Ella stumbled.

"She's an old woman, what can she do?" Scarlett pulled free and headed towards the cottage.

"You don't understand, she's not human."

She woke at dawn, once again soaked in sweat. "Neptune's shells, I thought that was behind me." She splashed cold water on her face and looked in the mirror. Dark circles ringed her eyes. "That was a lifetime ago."

The smell of freshly brewed tea wafted in, bringing her to life, and she went out to find a full pot seated on the counter, all snugged up in a cozy. Rumple was curled up on the sofa. As she pulled back the curtains, a chorus of loud annoyed sounding squeaks came from the kitchen. Her three little friends had been hard at work while she slept. She poured herself a cup of tea and found a plate of scrambled eggs and toast on the counter waiting for her.

"You lads are too good to me."

"We know," they said in unison.

She laughed and took her plate to her office.

Scarlett opened her laptop to see a dozen of messaged from BigBad1. Her grin was wolfish as she tapped the message screen. The messages were timestamped throughout the night.

Instead of responding to him, she put in a video call to Piper. The screen opened instantly, and Piper was, somehow, picture-perfect after working all night. Coal black feathers covered their head with dramatic bands of yellow eyeshadow around their golden eyes. Piper's face was narrow and had a large hawk-like nose and thin lips painted black. A silver choker with a crescent moon dangling from it adorned their neck over a purple silk blouse. With a twinge of jealousy, Scarlett looked at her friend and wished she knew their secret because this early in the day she looked like a bridge troll.

"Hey, you get anythin'?"

The three mice popped up on the desk next to her.

"Lou? Monty? Rodney? You look great!"

"So do you, Piper!"

Piper laughed. When not raging at Scarlett, Piper's voice was melodic, almost hypnotizing.

"He's not a tech savvy predator."

"You found him?"

"Of course, darling. You're paying for the best. Oh wait…"

"I'll owe you big time and this time I will actually pay."

"Mhmm."

"I can. Well, once I get paid."

"Well then, I guess I'll put in for my retirement now." Their smile took some of the sting from the barb.

"You should. My new client? He's very *charming*."

There was silence on the other end, then an almost whispered, "No way."

"Way. Now you know why I need your special skills."

"Listen, Red, I will always have your back."

"And I wouldn't blame you if you didn'"

Piper sighed. "Not going to pretend I was happy when you busted my partner for selling Pixie Dust out of our shop. That bad press almost killed it, but what really hurt? When you dipped and left me to deal with it all by myself."

"I'm sorry. I figured you hated me."

"Never. He was a slug and deserved it. But I could have used a friend. Someone to have *my* back."

"Sorry."

"Water, bridges, and all that. We've got a bigger fish to fry right now."

Scarlett smiled at the screen. She took a sip of tea to hide her sudden feelings of awkwardness. "You gonna spill the tea or what?"

Piper chuckled. It sounded almost like the gronking from her raven friend, Lokes. Which shouldn't be surprising, mynah birds and ravens were cousins. "Fine, fine. I found your BigBad1. His real name is Rolf Gernsback. He's thirty-eight. Not much history; moves around a lot. Birthplace shows as some town called Gruselige."

"Where do I know that name?"

"Not sure, darling, but there's more. For the last ten years, in every place he's lived there are reports of girls between fourteen and eighteen going missing. He moves and the disappearances stop."

"Any ever found?"

"Not alive."

"Neptune's shells."

"Indeed."

"We need to hurry."

"Agreed." Piper looked away for a second, then turned back. "Scarlett. Please be careful. This one's dangerous."

"So am I." She opened her desk drawer and removed her 9mil. "Thanks again. It's time for the predator to become the prey."

She disconnected the phone, took the cotton fluff from the mice's ears and filled them in.

"Got him," she said with a wolfish grin at her laptop.

"Need any 'elp this afternoon?"

"Spread the word, just in case he bolts."

"Will do," Lou said around a mouthful of scrambled eggs he'd stolen. With a final squeak, the three comrades disappeared down the fire escape.

She glanced at her watch, nine am. "No time like the present." She stood and tucked her gun into its shoulder holster, pulled on her signature red hoodie, and headed down the stairs.

Scarlett arrived at the address Piper had given her. She'd expected the GPS to lead to a warehouse or to the seedy part of town, but she found herself in the upscale financial district. "Your destination is on the right."

It was a tall four-storey building made of red brick, nestled in a row of other four-storey red brick buildings. Only the signage differentiated one from the other. The little bobbing marker on her phone pointed to Wolf in Sheep's Clothing Fashions. The door was locked and a glowing red sign in the window read "CLOSED". There had to be a back way in.

It was almost a full block away, but she found the alley.

"This is it. The back end of 21 Drury Lane." The famous muffin maker was across the street. She hid behind a garbage bin until the time she was to meet BigBad1 had passed. She climbed onto the bin and jumped to reach the bottom rung of the fire escape. Hand over hand she climbed looking for a way inside, finding each window was locked or bordered over.

"Neptune's shells." She climbed on. "One left." The top floor window was grimy but already open a crack and fine scrape marks marred the sill.

She wiggled the window open and into an empty hall with two doors. She pulled out her gun and went to the first door. It was an empty office. The other door opened to a large empty room filled with the reek of death. It was all around her. Bile rose in her throat. Four large, hard plastic dog crates that were bolted to the floor sat against the opposite wall. She checked each one in turn. Three were empty but the last one had a pile of rags in the back. Then the rags moved, and a pair of sky-blue eyes looked out at her.

"Calliope?"

"Yeah?"

"I'm Scarlett. Your grandfather hired me to find you."

"He did?"

Scarlett nodded and hit the lock with the butt of her gun. It was a cheap lock and shattered on the first blow.

Calliope crawled out. "Let's get out of here," Scarlett said.

They made their way to the door. "You said your name is Scarlett?"

"Yeah."

"Scarlett Hood?"

"That's me. Why?" She shot Calliope a look over her shoulder.

"He was looking for you."

"Who?" Scarlett stopped now and turned to face Calliope.

Calliope lifted her arm and pointed her finger behind Scarlett. "Him."

Scarlett spun. He stood at the door to the hallway. She'd never met him before, but she knew him instantly. Tall, muscular, and distinguished with touches of grey in his hair. He looked just like his mother. Scarlett's world spun.

The voice was deep, rough. Scarlett had entered the cottage and pushed open the bedroom door. The room was lit only by the weak moonlight shining through the window. It silhouetted the shape in the bed. it looked bigger than the old woman she'd seen. A pair of large luminous eyes shone in the moonlight.

"You aren't my Rolfy," the voice said.

Unconsciously Scarlett squeezed the axe handle. "My Grandma, what large eyes you have this evening."

"All the better to see you with."

Scarlett took a step back, bumping into Ella who was trying to see over her shoulder. "Scarlett, come on." She tugged Scarlett's arm.

A strange detachment came over Scarlett and held her in place. She could see the arms that held the blankets close. They were large and muscular with long, boney hands covered in coarse grey hair with long jagged nails.

"Oh Grandma, what large arms you have."

"All the better for hugging."

There was movement in the shadow and Grandma swung her feet over the edge of the bed and stood. Lean muscular legs stuck out from beneath her flower-covered flannel gown that only reached her knobby knees. She was taller and her face seemed distorted, squarer and a trick of the light made her look like she had a muzzle. She stepped from the shadows and smiled, thin grey lips pulled back revealing a set of fearsome canines. Scarlett froze. "Neptune's shells, Grandma, what freakishly large teeth you have."

Grandmother laughed. It sounded like a growl. "All the better to eat you with, my dear." Muscles bunched and she dove at Scarlett, teeth bared and claws extended. Ella screamed and stumbled backward. Without thinking, Scarlett brought up the axe and swung. It hit with a sickening thunk. An animal scream shook the small cottage.

Scarlett pulled the axe free and ran from the cottage. Ella was already halfway across the field. She could certainly move for an octogenarian. She bolted down the steps and onto the path. A howl came from behind her, and she felt a burning pain in her left shoulder. She hit the ground hard, the wind blasted from her lungs and the axe flying from her grasp. She wiggled and twisted, trying to dislodge the weight of Grandma. They rolled down a small incline, arms and legs flying, fists punching. When they hit the bottom, Scarlett found herself on her back with Grandmother on top. She fought to free herself, bucking her hips and trying to knee her in the back but the old woman's claws bit deep into the flesh of her arms, and she cried out in pain.

"What are you?"

"I'm not a what but a were." She laughed that growling chuckle. "A werewolf to be exact."

"Werewolves aren't real."

The old woman lowered her face to inches above Scarlett's. Her breath smelled like an abattoir, and saliva dripped from her fangs onto Scarlett's face. She turned away in disgust.

"We're not monsters to scare children with, we're just trying to survive. For generations we hunted for our food, leaving you humans in peace. Now you've hunted our prey to near extinction, destroyed our hunting grounds and dens." Scarlett caught a look of sadness flicker over Grandmother's face. "We take what we need to survive, as we always did." Grandmother's teeth plunged down and Scarlett turned her face away.

Warmth splattered her face and there was a sickening thunk and grunt. Something heavy landed on her and then was gone. She opened her eyes to see Ella standing above her, silhouetted against the full moon, a bloody axe in her hand.

"Come now. We go home."

"Rolf."

"Ms. Hood." He tipped his head in acknowledgment. "You stood me up. How'd you find my den?"

Scarlett's lips twitched. "A little birdie told me. Now your turn, why?"

"An eye for an eye and all that."

"You could have found and killed me without all this. Why the kids?"

"Oh that? That was just sport."

"None of this makes sense." She shook her head.

"Why Calliope? How'd you know Charming would come to me?"

"Old man Charming and I go way back. Said he had a deadbeat grandkid. Thought I'd help him with that. You were just a bonus." He gave a shudder and the two watched in horror as he morphed from man to beast. His hair became wiry, and his face extended into a stumpy muzzle with long fangs hanging below his lips. His shoulders moved forward, and nails grew into claws. "I plan on enjoying this."

"What… what…" Calliope's voice failed her.

"Back to the crate. Hide."

"No. I can't," Calliope said. "I'd sooner die than be caged again."

Rolf's voice was guttural: "But that's just what you'd do to us."

Scarlett scoffed. "You're killing children."

"To survive and only the weak; drug users, prostitutes, sick in body or mind."

"They're children."

"They're prey." He moved quickly, almost faster than she could track. She fired. A miss. It ricocheted off the wall in a puff of red brick powder and drywall.

"She has teeth," he said as he ran. In a blur of motion, she felt a burn and looked down to see blood blossoming on her jeans, torn flesh beneath. She cried out and clamped a hand over the wound. Her gun shook. Another rush, another wound. This time across her ribs. She fired again, but he was no longer where she'd been aiming. He was playing with her. A cat with a mouse.

Behind her, from the direction of the alley, she heard

a noise. She acknowledged it but was too focused on surviving the next few minutes to worry. Attack after attack came and went. She had half a dozen hits from him but none on him, but she didn't care. She was within two feet of the door.

"Calliope," she whispered over her shoulder. "When I say, open that door and run out the window, down the fire escape. Just go. Don't look back."

He stopped his run, poised, tense. He gave her time to aim. A false sense of hope. She had one bullet left.

Close enough, she thought.

"Go," she said; and Calliope went.

Time slowed. She heard the click of the latch opening as she saw him coil to leap. The rush of air as the door opened ruffled her hair and the soft sounds of a flute carried on the breeze. Her eyes were locked on him, her thumb reached for the hammer. So focused was she that she almost missed it, the sounds of hundreds of feet running. The rustle of feathers. His eyes went wide, and a roar escaped his throat as he leapt at her, teeth bared.

Hundreds of furry and feathered bodies hit him mid-leap, driving him to the floor. They swarmed him. Teeth biting, sharp beaks probing. Scarlett glanced over her shoulder and saw three mice of unusual size with cotton wool in their ears and a person with raven feathers for hair playing the flute. "Pop's flute finally came in handy."

Calliope stood frozen between them. "Go with them," Scarlett told her. She turned back to Piper. "Get her out."

They poked the flute into their breast pocket and held out a hand to Calliope, but spoke to Scarlett. "Red, that's another you owe me."

"Add it to the list."

She turned back to the seething mass of feathers and fur. She raised the gun as he threw her small allies away. Bleeding from hundreds of bites, he stood panting before her.

"Lead? You think lead will kill me?"

She pulled back the hammer. "Nope. But silver should do the trick."

Scarlett pulled her red cloak close as she took the elevator to her new office in Charming Towers. She stood before the door listening to conversations coming from inside. Piper's melodic tones above the squeaky voices of the mice. She smiled and ran her fingers over the gold paint: "Hood and Associates — Wolf Hunters."

Lisa M Daly

Lisa M Daly is an archaeologist, historian, professional ballroom dance instructor, crafter, and avid baker.

Previous non-fiction writing credits include essays *Sacrifice in Second World War Gander* and *An Empty Graveyard: The Victims of the 1946 AOA DC-4 Crash, Their Final Resting Place*, and *Dark Tourism*.

She made her fiction writing debut with "The Island Outside the War" in *Dystopia from the Rock*.

Lisa acted as the guest editor for the Summer 2019 *Flights from the Rock* collection.

In 2021 she released her first novella, *Navigating Stories*.

The Three Sisters

Act 1

The door slammed open, and their father walked in with a very non-descript man behind him.

"Welcome John, or was it Jack? Either way, welcome!" the father loudly proclaimed.

The three sisters looked up. The eldest was held a quill up to sheet of music. She made the notation, then put the quill back in the pot. The dulcimer in front of her sat quietly, waiting for the next note. The middle sister finished pulling a thread through her fabric, and rested the needle and the fabric on her lap. The youngest sister put aside her book.

"You have slain the dragon, and now you will have your choice of my daughters," the large man said with a magnanimous wave of his hand.

"The dragon is dead?" the eldest asked.

"Wait, what?" the middle sister asked.

"Father, who is this man?" the youngest asked.

Ignoring his daughters, the father continued. "Please choose your reward."

Jack, or maybe John, an average man of average stature, looked at the three sisters and started toward the youngest.

The eldest sister stood up quickly. "What do you think you are doing?" she cried. "Choose me to gain land," she said.

John or Jack, a man of no distinguishing features, moved closer to the youngest daughter, reached out, and grabbed her hand.

The middle sister stood, holding the tapestry needle she had been working with. The tread slipped through the needle and fell to the floor. She walked over to the man and stabbed the needle into the hand holding her sister, electing a grunt of pain from him.

"What the hell is your problem," she snarled. "She is a child, barely sixteen. You get your hand off her."

Jack, or John, pulled his hand back, the needle ripping as it pulled free. He would have a scar, something people might remember about it. Holding his bleeding hand, his eyes darted wildly between the three sisters before he fled through the open door, having never said a word.

The youngest, Kalissa, wiped at her eyes as tears started to well.

"What is wrong with you girls?" the father bellowed, taking a step towards them. "He saved our kingdom from the dragon! He deserves an award."

The eldest, Hedya, stood. She ripped her music off the stand and jammed it into a satchel. She grabbed the lute that was resting by the wall.

"The dragon was peaceful, Father. You know I would spend hours at his cave writing songs and stories about his centuries of life." She brushed past her father and walked out the door.

The middle daughter, Samena, picked up her bag of fabrics and threads. "We are not rewards. You could have offered money or land. We are not prizes." She pushed past and joined her sister outside.

The two sisters watched from the open doorway, waiting to see if either their sister would move or their father would stop her. Kalissa wiped her tears and stood, picking up her book. "I will be a princess, not a prize," she said, and scurried past to join her sisters.

Outside, they looked at each other. Their father started to bellow, once again choosing words over actual action; and so, as one, they turned away and started down the lane.

The cobblestones of the manor home gave way to packed dirt. Hedya hesitated just slightly on the threshold, glanced behind her, checked her posture, and stepped off the stones. Her sisters smiled as they continued on.

Act 2

The lane divided, turning into the town or the road to the next town.

"Where should we go?" Hedya asked. "The town is closer."

"The town is also full of people who would return us to our father in exchange for forgiveness of even a little debt." Samena considered for a moment. "No, we continue on."

"But we have no food or water," Kalissa whined.

"Lunch was not yet an hour ago," Samena reminded her. "The next town is only a two hour's walk. We will be fine."

"And how will we pay for food when we get to the next town? Here we could pay with father's credit," Hedya pointed out.

Samena indicated Hedya's lute. "Why did you take the lute if not to play?"

"I took it because Mother gave it to me," Hedya explained, looking at the instrument in her hands. Even the thought of their late mother brought a mix of heaviness and peace to her heart.

"Then Mother would say to play it," Samena suggested.

"I have never played outside of a recital…" Hedya argued.

"You could play now as we walk!" Kalissa suggested with a smile as bright as the day around them.

"I suppose…" Hedya hesitated, then adjusted her satchel and made as if to play, tuning the strings as they walked down the path toward the next town.

She played quietly at first, humming softly with the song, but then, as her fingers found their rhythm, and as she learned how to walk and play, she began to pluck louder, singing clearly enough for her sisters to hear. When Samena and Kalissa started to sing the chorus, they all got louder. Soon, they were walking and singing, and enjoying their travel.

As they were approaching a farmhouse, they heard a voice boom. "What is that caterwauling? Must you abuse the sanctity of others' ears?" called an old man sitting on the stoop.

Hedya hesitated, then stopped playing. Samena and Kalissa went on singing despite the lack of accompaniment. As the chorus ended, the women fell silent in front of the house, and the man looked at them smugly.

"That's better. No more disturbing the peace," he said, satisfied.

Hedya picked a string on her lute. He glared. She picked another. As he opened his mouth to say something, she broke into a song:

What right have you, to stop our joy
You drown our voices with you own
Loud, intimidating
You are disturbing our peace
And we will no longer be silent.
Rise up, soft voices,
Rise up and sing
We can speak to
Let your voices ring!

She sang the second part again, and Samena and Kalissa joined in. The man tried to speak over them, but the three sang louder, and carried on down the road, Samena throwing an obscene gesture back at the man, then stifling a laugh as she saw him get up to shake a fist at her.

The sisters continued to walk and sing for the next few hours before finding a town for the night.

Entering the town, they were still singing, Hedya repeating the verses she was creating to better commit them to memory. Passing an inn, a woman sweeping the stoop paused and listened until they reached the end.

"That's quite the tune; I think it will go over well with my patrons. I'll give the three of you a room if you'll perform tonight," she said.

Hedya hesitated. "That's my only original song," she

admitted.

"But it's one my patrons will love. You know others?" she asked, and Hedya nodded. "Good. Play some of the others, but break that one out a few times throughout the night."

Hedya still looked uncertain, but her sisters both gave her encouraging smiles.

"Very well, I'll do it," Hedya said drawing confidence from her sisters' belief.

"Good. I'm Libelle and this is the Well-Dressed Ale," she said, tapping the sign above the door of a foaming mug wearing a skirt. "Come in and get cleaned up. Dinner is in an hour, then you'll sing after that."

The sisters followed Libelle inside.

Hours later, Hedya was still singing, and the room was singing with her.

Rise up, soft voices,
Rise up and sing
We can speak to
Let your voices ring!

She had lost count of how often she had sung the song, but the women in the room kept asking for it and singing along every time. By now, most in the room knew the whole song. And the room was mostly women. Libelle had explained that her common room was somewhere for women to get a drink without having to worry about roaming hands or unwanted attention. Any man who came in either respected the rules or would be refused service. Kalissa had never seen anything like this place, full of women dressed in every colour of the rainbow, enjoying drinks and singing. They were all at ease and comfortable in the space, with the threats of the outside world at bay while they sang about having a voice.

The next morning, Hedya nursed a cup of honeyed tea to soothe her tired voice. Samena and Kalissa sat at the table, Kalissa with her doll and Samena with her stitching. Libelle carried a tray of bread, cheese, and meats to their table and sat down with them.

"Last night was amazing!" Libelle said, helping herself to some of the food. "I have never seen a song take off so quickly."

Kalissa chewed thoughtfully on a piece of cheese. "Libelle," she asked. "How did you create this place? We haven't been traveling long, but we have never seen anything like this."

"It was my grandmother's dream, a place for all women to have and enjoy," Libelle answered.

"But there were men here too," Kalissa pointed out.

"Yes, some men, but only those who respect female space. There were also those who are neither men nor women who want a space. As long as you are respectful of people's identity and space, you are welcome here," Libelle explained.

"That could almost be another song," Hedya croaked.

"Not until your voice recovers," Samena admonished, popping a piece of meat into her mouth before picking up her needle again.

Hedya smiled and sipped her tea.

After breakfast, Libelle gave them some food, and a few coins. "We made a lot of money last night," she explained. "This is your share for keeping everyone singing throughout the night. If you're ever in town again, I would be happy to host you." She waved them off as they walked out of town.

Weeks passed, and the sisters walked. Hedya wrote and practiced more songs and played for their beds in the towns they passed through. She sang the songs she wrote in the dragon's cave, and others she wrote on the road. One song was always requested, and soon she found that people, especially women, already knew the words to her song, for it was passing from town to town ahead of them. With the opening notes, taverns full of people would sing along:

Rise up, soft voices,
Rise up and sing
We can speak to
Let your voices ring!

Hedya was not just paying for their rooms with her voice, but making money, their pockets growing heavy with the coin she earned. She gave Samena money for needle work supplies and bought books for Kalissa. Each evening, Samena would find the quietest corner possible and stitch, while Kalissa talked with tavern patrons. One day, they had stopped in a larger town when Hedya looked at her sisters over their lunch.

"Sisters, I think I have decided what I want to do. I can make a living writing songs. In a place like this, with so many taverns and pubs, I can maybe settle for a while," Hedya explained. "My feet are weary from the road, and I think I would like a home of my own."

"What about us?" Samena asked.

"You are welcome to stay here too," Hedya suggested.

"I don't think I've yet figured out what I want to do," Samena admitted.

"What about you, Kalissa?" Hedya asked.

Kalissa considered. "No. I want to be a princess. And I cannot be a princess here."

Hedya and Samena smiled at her the way all older sisters smile at their younger siblings. "Then I guess we will continue on. We will write frequently," Samena said with a decisive nod before she picked up her embroidery.

Weeks passed on the road. Samena and Kalissa would stop at towns and hear Hedya's songs performed by other people, and felt her love following them through her words. As always, they joined in with the crowd:

Rise up, soft voices,
Rise up and sing
We can speak to
Let your voices ring!

Act 3

One evening, sitting in a shadowy tavern, the candlelight casting shadows over her fabric, Samena listened to another rendition of her sister's song. Kalissa was at another table, discussing something with a group of local residents. Samena drew her needle through the fabric and looked up to find a woman in a kerchief sitting across from her.

"Do you take commissions?" the woman asked, wringing her hands around a crumpled piece of paper.

"I'm not sure that myself and my sister will be here long enough for a commission," Samena admitted, glancing at her sister's animated conversation.

"Can you work something into this piece, then?" she asked, indicating the needlework.

Samena turned the work over in her hands. It was a pattern of red flowers in a basket, more than half-stitched.

"I could, as long as it's not too elaborate..." Samena replied.

The woman released a breath and flattened the paper on the table. "This letter came from the vicar's wife two towns over. She expresses concern for my sister's safety. She says, 'Karlie, please help your sister before she commits a terrible sin. Please send word, Raene.' My sister, Leoda, can't read or write, but if you could add a Christmas rose to the middle, along with some juniper and Queen Anne's lace?"

Samena took a lead from her kit and sketched the flowers into the pattern. "Like this?" she asked, turning the fabric toward Karlie.

She beamed. "Yes, just like that."

Samena looked at the pattern. "I don't understand," she admitted.

Karlie gave her a quizzical look. "You don't know the language of flowers? The rose asks her to relieve my anxiety, the juniper offers protection, and the Queen Anne's lace is offering haven. She will get her husband to help her write a letter and she will draw her actual response in the margins," Karlie explained.

Samena paused and looked at the pattern again. "We are planning on continuing north, so I can finish it and deliver it to her as we pass," she offered, curious and invested enough to see the story through.

Karlie clapped her hands, "Oh, would you? Thank

you!" She reached into her skirts and withdrew a small pouch. She pulled some coins from the bag and placed them on the table. "Coin for the work, and coin for delivery."

Samena tried to protest, but Karlie pushed the coins across the table. "And coin for your help in keeping my sister safe."

Lastly, she pressed a fold of paper into Samena's hand. "Thank you," Karlie whispered once more, then turned and disappeared into the crowd.

Kalissa appeared and took Karlie's place. "What is all of this?" she asked, eyeing the coins and Samena's bewilderment.

Samena looked at her sister, "I'm going to be running a coded message."

A few days later, Samena knocked nervously on the door. A large man opened, and a young woman hovered just behind him.

"What!" he demanded, his voice a boom that reminded Samena uncomfortably of her father.

She hesitated, the straightened. "This is for Leoda. Karlie asked me to drop it off as we passed through."

The brute swiped the piece of fabric. "What is this?" he demanded.

"Just an embroidery piece I made. I was working on it when I met Karlie." Carla spoke past the man to Leoda. "It's just a basket of flowers like Christmas rose, juniper, and Queen Anne's lace. Your sister thought you would like it."

With heavy hands, he turned it over. Satisfied it was just flowers, he threw it at Leoda, harrumphed, and started to close the door.

"Karlie hopes you will write to her soon," Samena called, making the briefest eye contact with the trembling woman who was delicately touching the French knots of the Queen Anne's lace.

That evening, at yet another tavern with yet another mug of ale, Samena stretched another piece of linen into a hoop. She picked up her lead and considered her next pattern when a woman with pinned dark hair gently streaked with silver sat down and placed a small book on the table.

Samena looked at the title. *The Language of Flowers*, it read.

"Thank you for contacting Leoda. Karlie wrote to me and asked me to give you this," she said, indicating the book. "And this." She reached across and pinned a dried rose leaf backed by a sprig of maidenhair fern to Samena's bodice. "It says you give hope but are discrete," the woman explained.

Samena looked down at the small leaflets of the fern backing the jagged rose leaf, then put her hand over the small book. "Thank you," she whispered.

The woman that she believed was Raene, the vicar's wife, placed her hand over Samena's. "Thank you for helping sweet Leoda. I hope you will choose to help others," she said, before removing her hand, pushing back her chair, and walking out of the tavern.

Samena lifted up the small book and started to look through the pages. There were line drawings of flowers, each with meanings corresponding to the colour. Toward the back of the delicate book, there was a list of stitch combinations in wool creations to spell out messages.

"What do you have?" Kalissa asked, reappearing at the table with more ale.

Samena explained with something that felt like destiny settling across her shoulders with every word.

The pin worked wonders. Within an hour of settling into an inn or tavern, women would come looking for Samena. When the dried leaves on her pin started to crumble from wear, she embroidered herself a new broach. She kept a collection of individual flower patterns: daffodils for unrequited love, motherwort for secret love, but also goldenrod for caution, and maidenhair for discretion. These could be sold on small scraps of fabric, perfect to paste to a card. Kalissa could always tell when someone was coming to talk to Samena about flowers and would leave the table, easily falling into conversation with another group, whether sailors, mothers, or nobles. Samena envied her ability to converse, and still felt awkward as each woman told her tale, her practicality sometimes hiding her empathy.

After many long roads and covert encounters in shadowed taverns, they came to an inn at the edge of a town. Kalissa had noted aloud that the towns were getting larger the further north they traveled. This particular inn was brighter than their usual haunts, with lily of the valley and Queen Anne's lace in the window boxes, and juniper bushes with white berries under the windows. Through the windows, they could see a brightly lit tearoom with one table occupied by well-dressed women picking at a tiered tower of small cakes and sandwiches.

"I don't think I'll find much clientele here, but it might be nice to stay somewhere fancy," Samena mused.

"Dear sister," Kalissa said, looking at the flower boxes and feeling out her instincts, "I think you'll be surprised." She stepped forward and opened the front door.

A woman in a pink dress came out from behind a dark wooden counter. She clasped her white-gloved hands together at the sight of them. "Welcome, welcome!" she said cheerfully. "We've been expecting you."

The sisters looked at each other: Samena in confusion while Kalissa gave her a reassuring smile.

"I'm Sofia. And you must be Kalissa and Samena. Oh, we've been waiting to meet you. No, no," Sofia waved off Samena just as she opened her mouth to ask a question. "First, you must be road weary, so I insist you get cleaned up. I will have a tray sent to your room."

SofiaShe led them up a long staircase to shuffle them to a room filled with pink ruffles and a pair of washbasins covered in blue flowers and full of steaming water.

"Whina will be up with a tray and I will be by to collect you shortly. You will find clothing in the cupboard. It may not be exactly your usual style, but I am convinced you will like it well enough," Sofia said as she backed out to the room.

Samena looked at her sister. "I don't understand," she admitted.

"I believe you are being recruited," Kalissa answered with a cheeky smile.

Soon the two women found themselves clothed in lace and frills, though in the darker colours that hid road dust and mud that they had come to prefer on their travels. Whina, the young girl who had brought them food earlier, knocked and guided them to the tearoom. More women were there than before, spread over a couple of tables. Kalissa was whisked off to one where the group started an animated chat, and she quickly fell into the conversation. Samena was seated at another table, where women were much more hushed, leaning together slightly in a conspiratorial manner.

"We've seen your work," Sofia opened. "It's very good, and the say you hide messages within patterns is some of the best."

Samena, feeling the confusion leave slightly, smiled shyly.

"But it's clear you have no training in espionage. You are much too visible and will get caught," hissed a white-haired, stern looking woman.

"Ella," Sofia scolded. "We discussed that we would speak softly to her, not scare her away."

Samena, chastened, wrang her hands. Sofia reached over to still her hands. "Don't worry about Ella, my dead. She can be gruff, but she is one of the best at what she does and will make a good teacher." Samena looked at Sofia and saw only kindness. Sofia continued, "You have a talent, but need better guidance. You need to learn to be more covert and how to make your messages say more, sometimes with less. What it comes down to, is that we hope you will join us."

"Join you in what?" Samena asked, still uncertain what was happening.

"In being a spy!" Kalissa called from her table.

Heads turned, and Kalissa beamed at her sister, completely unrepentant. .

"Your sister sees a lot," Ella said. "She is a bit of a force."

Samena laughed and smiled at Kalissa, letting her fondness overcome her embarrassment. "Yes, she is. She's been leading us along this path for a while."

"I don't doubt it. We'll hear more from her," Ella said, matter-of-factly.

"She is right," Sofia said. "We have been helping women for generations. Helping them escape abusive marriages, helping them find work, and passing messages to sympathetic men in power to pass rules and laws to better the lives of women. Basically, we hope you'll keep doing what you are doing, but sometimes help in bigger ways."

"I will miss you, Kalissa. Where will you go?" Samena asked.

"Where I've been heading since we left. I am going north to the palace. I will be a princess," she answered frankly.

"Of course you will. I hope to hear from you soon. Here, this is for you," Samena said, handing her an embroidery. It was their names, Hedya, Samena, and Kalissa, surrounded by white carnations and white heather. "This is a gift of luck, protection, and hope that your dreams will come true."

Kalissa hugged her sister. "Thank you so much. I will write as soon as I can."

Act 4

Kalissa set off out of town on her own. She had plenty of coin given to her by her sisters to reach her destination. Walking, her journey was still slow, but walking gave her time to grow. She would talk to merchants and farmers, adventurers and holiday makers; she would converse with every traveler she met, learning their stories and sharing news. She ate at kitchen tables in exchange for stories from afar, and had drinks paid for while enjoying discussions of business and markets.

She heard Hedya's songs sung in many taverns and town squares. She learned to spot the meetings and messages between women, working to protect each other, and thought she could recognize Samena's stitches now and then. She had always heard of how the world was said to work, but now could finally observe how it actually worked.

She kept walking, the towns getting larger the closer she got, shifting from townships to cities. Eventually, she came to a large walled city, and passed through the gate with other travelers. The city was huge, with buildings packed tightly together and large crowds of people busily moving through the streets. Kalissa walked, and as the buildings started to spread out, she picked somewhere to stay for the night.

The inn was dark, the windows shuttered, but Kalissa saw a needlework offering protection and continued to the desk. She decided it was a perfect place to spend the night.

The next morning, she left the inn to walk deeper into

the city. As the buildings spaced themselves out more, the tenements gave way to small, individual townhouses with gates and brightly coloured sashes. The shops changed as well, from shonky shops to general stores then boutiques as the houses became larger. She stopped to make a few purchases, new clothing and shoes for her to wear in the city instead of her road-tired clothes. Soon, she selected a hotel within view of the palace and asked for a room.

The clerk eyed her clothing and shoes, and her tattered bag and sniffed.

Before he could say anything, Kalissa added, "I also believe some packages have been delivered for me."

Giving her name, the clerk made a show of checking an adjacent room, and then remarkably, his attitude changed completely. He called for a bellhop to bring the boxes of clothing to Kalissa's room, indicating he should not allow her to carry her own bags.

"I also need hot water for washing; is a bath available?" she asked with a charming smile.

The clerk readily agreed and gave a few more orders to staff. With a little money and the name of minor nobility from a far-away county, Kalissa went from being an urchin to a lady, quickly gaining all of the privileges associated with her station.

The following morning, she called for a maid to help her dress and style her own hair. Over her time traveling, Kalissa was used to doing these things herself, but her new clothes were designed to require help dressing. Once outside, she considered ordering a carriage and arriving in style, but then decided she had come this far on foot, so she would finish by walking.

At the palace gates, Kalissa was allowed to pass without question. At the entrance, she gave her name to the doorman, who allowed her to enter and led her to a waiting chamber. After some time alone, she was brought to the throne room where the king and queen sat in their thrones. Others milled around, mostly footmen, but also some nobility. A couple of people wore smaller crowns, so she took them to be the princes and princesses of the kingdom.

"Young miss, I have not heard from your county in some time. Are you here to bring a message from your father?" the king asked.

"Goodness no," Kalissa replied. "Myself and my sisters left my father's home many moons ago, vowing to never return."

"If you do not have a missive for me, then why are you here? I only allowed you in to give word from your father," the king scolded.

The queen cut in, "Now dear, this young woman seems to have a tale to tell." She turned to Kalissa. "Why would you leave your father's home?"

"Your majesty," Kalissa said with a brief curtsey. "I left because he was going to give me as a reward to a man who killed a peaceful dragon."

The king scoffed. "Dragons are rarely peaceful, and it is custom to offer a boon to a slayer of dragons."

"I assure you this one was peaceful. Myself and my sisters all spent time with him. As for a boon, my father was too cheap to give land or money, so instead offered up his daughters," Kalissa replied, careful to keep her voice respectful. She was drawing the attention of the court for daring to speak so to the king.

"Such is a worthy reward. Young women need suitors," the king replied.

"What of young men?" she retorted. "Can I ask for the hand of one of the princes?"

The king laughed. "And what have you done to merit such a thing?"

"I have walked from my father's home and have learned of this kingdom. I have learned that to the south the taxes are too high and it inhibits farmers from meeting their grain quotas. I have learned that the merchants on the coast refuse to follow the guidelines set by the crown, and only pay the lowest prices for fish, no matter the quality. I have learned that women throughout this kingdom have networks to keep each other safe when they are at risk from their fathers and husbands. And I have learned that only the women of the population get treated as items of trade, while men can be much freer." Agnes spoke loud and clear, thinking of Hedya's singing voice. "I have also learned that somehow, men can walk into a home and ask for a woman's hand in marriage based only on her age and looks, but if I were to do that in this room, I would likely be laughed away or thrown in jail for my presumption."

The king looked strongly displeased with Kalissa's speech, but the queen quieted him again. before she stood. "Is that what you wish, Miss Kalissa, to marry one of my sons?" she asked.

"My whole life, young as I am, I have dreamed of being a princess. After seeing so much, I decided that I would simply come here and ask. I will not slay a dragon, but I will talk to merchants and negotiate better working conditions for your people, and that is a greater threat to the health of this land."

The queen laughed a little. "Very well," she said, then raised her voice so it would carry around the room. "My sons, we were to start looking for suitable wives for you, and this young woman have come to take your hand. She makes a fair point. When your eldest sisters came of age, suitors could walk into the palace and make their case for marriage. I see no reason why she cannot do the same. Now, come forth if you would like to wed Kalissa here, from a minor lineage far on the outskirts of our kingdom."

The queen looked around the room, which was silent. Soon, some of the nobles snickered quietly, mocking Kalissa grand gesture.

"Very well—" the queen started.

"I will come forward," said one of the young men, pushing himself up to his feet.

"Nonsense," scoffed the king. "You are the heir to the throne. You cannot decide to marry a woman who walks in here and throws such an outburst at the feet of the court."

"Have you not listened to her, Father?" the prince asked. "She has been talking to our people and has learned about our land. You only talk to nobles and the few who dare to petition you, knowing you will always take the side of the nobles and merchants. Multiple times, I have heard fishermen complain of the merchants, and women complain of being mere possessions."

"I make decisions based on the needs of this land," the

king argued, growing red in the face.

"No," the prince retorted. "You make decisions in favour of those you feel are more important and more worthy. It's why we had to quell a strike to the west and there are still complaints to the south. Is it not her father's lands from where farmers have been sending petitioners to do something about the high taxes?"

"You still have many years left before you are king, but I will not see you destroy my kingdom before then," the king retorted.

"Father, I will not say I will marry this woman right now, but I would like to learn what she knows. I have never been outside the city walls, and even then, it has been very controlled." He turned to Kalissa. "If I may ask, will you stay at the palace and teach me of this land so that, when it is time, I will be a better ruler? I will not promise you marriage but would like to get to know you better."

Kalissa's goal was to be a princess, but she decided that being an advisor to the crown prince, with a chance of becoming a princess, was a better prospect... And so she accepted with a gracious lowering of her head and a smile.

Eve Morton

Eve Morton is a Canadian writer living in Waterloo, Ontario.

When she is not teaching online classes or working on yet another project, Eve is often reading a lot of books or listening to music from some of her favourite artists. She also loves to explore New Age shops in each city she visits whenever she travels, and continues to read tarot and astrology. She continues to do academic research on LGBTQ communities, pulp and genre fiction, and film studies, along with other academic issues involving addiction, mental illness, and student representation.

She has published three books to date: *The Serenity Nearby* (Sapphire), *Holidays in Blue* (Carina Press), and *The Twilight Kingdom* (JMS Books). She brings with her her short story 'Pinochino's Puppet'.

Pinochio's Puppet

It was just her luck.

The moment she transformed into a real boy, she wanted to be a girl. She *was* a girl. That was truly what Pinocchio had learned inside the belly of the whale and on Pleasure Island with all those rough kids. Oh boy, was she not one of them. Not in the very least.

She was a girl.

Even when she'd been a donkey, she'd still been a girl.

And she wanted to go home again.

That was why she went back to Geppetto. She figured that, with the help of the Blue Fairy and her always present conscience, the old carpenter could give Pinocchio what she wanted. Wasn't that the wish, too? The happy ending to the fairy tale? Her true self? Though her human nose would no longer give her away, she was still devoted to truth.

So she returned. She said the magic words. She waited for her world to change.

But her body betrayed her. Her skin became rough with the splinters of beard hair that would grow in the future. Her chest was flat as a board. Her hair was dark mahogany in color, like another piece of furniture in Geppetto's workroom, and as coarse and knotted as a piece of driftwood.

Was this the truth? It couldn't be. She was about to turn to the fairy to give her a piece of her newly minted mind, when the little voice whispered in her ear, "Give it time."

"What?"

"My son!" Geppetto reached his arms around her body and hugged her close. "My son. My heir. The one and only Pinocchio."

Pinocchio — she had never really minded the name — eased into the hug. Geppetto's shoulder blades were sharp and present under his skin. His hair fell out in tuffs, grey mixing with the dark blue on his carpenter's uniform. He smelled like wood, but also like the fetid scent of the forest after a rainstorm, thick with decay. Geppetto was old. Geppetto was going to die soon.

"Give it time," the small voice whispered again in Pinocchio's ear. "Everything will come to you in time."

Pinocchio whipped her dark hair around to try and find the little cricket but saw nothing. Even the Blue Fairy had deserted her, and once again, she figured that was just her luck. Hadn't she seen a glimmer of pink against the fairy's neck, so much like stubble? Hadn't she been too tall and too majestic to ever have been anything but a true fairy and a drag queen? Pinocchio needed her — for makeup tips alone — but she still had this little problem in front of her.

Geppetto was petting her hair, short and tucked under

the ridiculous cap she was wearing as part of the puppet uniform.

It would need to be the first thing to go.

"Yes, Daddy," she said as she gripped the old man's arms and told him what he wanted to hear — for now. "It's me, your boy. Love you, too. So can we talk about a different outfit?"

Days passed and Pinocchio slowly adjusted to her new body. Being human — rather than a puppet — came with it several new experiences that she had to nail down before concerning herself with anything else.

Like using the bathroom. She was pretty sure that even if she had been gifted the body she wanted, that using a toilet would have baffled her. Using diapers was not the solution, though Geppetto insisted that he could sew as well as twist wood to his desires, and so he could make her some cloth diapers like he'd made her current unisex jumpsuit. She quickly declined another kind gift and became determined to learn this skill by herself and right away. Even at the cost of eating, which was another strange thing she needed to master.

Her hunger was intense by the time she got around to her first true meal. Snacks — and truly, all experiences on Pleasure Island — didn't count. They had been done for fancy, not for survival. Her hunger seemed to linger no matter how much she ate or tried to stave it off. Strange and persistent — so much like her feeling that she had been given the wrong body.

"You're just a growing boy," Geppetto said when she

sheepishly asked for three servings at dinner. He heaped rice and corn onto her plate and gave her another cut of meat, though the carpenter could barely afford it. "Ah, you'll eat me out of house and home. It's what I expected, having a boy."

Pinocchio's face fell as she accepted the new plate. Lying was yet another thing she was getting used to. At first, it was a novel sensation to no longer be haunted by her nose, but she soon grew weary of avoiding her truth. How could no one else see it? She was a girl, man. A total girl.

But in the glimmer of a spoon, she saw a different truth. She flipped it over and didn't pick it up again.

Pinocchio continued to pick at her dinner before asking, "What did you expect if you had a girl? Would you have wanted a girl?"

The little voice spoke over Geppetto's answer: "Give it time."

"Excuse me?" Pinocchio said. "What was that?"

"I didn't want a girl," Geppetto replied. His sour expression was not exactly mean, or misogynistic — a word Pinocchio had read in a recent book — but it wasn't neutral, either. Eventually, he let out a long sigh that ended with, "Girls only leave."

"Oh." Pinocchio felt something flicking at her ear. She batted it away, then pretended to curl her dark hair in her fingers. "I don't have to leave, you know."

"Right. You'll be my heir. So, you'll bring your wife, and your babies, here." Geppetto gestured away from the quaint dining room and down the hallway where his workroom was.

Pinocchio had spent a lot of time in the workroom

while learning her basic human tasks. She liked the smell of the varnish and pine; the texture and feel of the half-finished pieces; and she absolutely adored the way in which some of the sawdust from projects glimmered in the afternoon light. Geppetto had recently replaced a window, and so glass tools had joined his others along the shelves. She loved the room. She loved the little lessons he gave her between projects, and how he stood protectively at her back as she touched the table saw for the first time. He loved her. He loved his work.

But she would never be the same to him, if she became the woman she wanted to be. He would watch her marry a man — but who was to say that she even liked men, especially after her time in Pleasure Island? — and then he'd most likely die of a broken heart as she left him.

Pinocchio sighed. She flipped corn on her fork, and once again, she heard the little voice in her head, "Give it time."

"Everything alright, my son?" Geppetto asked.

"Yeah, Dad. Just thinking of my next woodworking project," she answered.

"Well, good. As long as it's not a crib." He smiled, but then it fell away from his face. "Though I do think that you're growing up awful fast."

"It happens when you're human."

"Yes," he said with a laugh. "Suppose it does."

About a month later, Pinocchio had mastered enough skills to take over a blank workspace close to Geppetto's. The final test had been a birdhouse she built with her father, followed by painting the various birds he loved on its sides. She'd had no idea Geppetto was so into finches, but he'd provided for her a dozen drawn pictures, and one taxidermized bird, so she had something to work from. In the back of her mind, she wondered if he'd had a dozen pictures of young boys in order to get her arms and legs exactly right.

Probably not, she thought bitterly. *Because he didn't get me exactly right.*

Whenever she failed in her finch-painting task, and had to start all over again, she expected Geppetto to be upset. To take over. She wasn't living up to her role as his son, so wouldn't he be angry?

But he simply put a hand on her back and told her she'd improve with time.

"Give it time," he said. "We all need time to be great at anything."

Pinocchio stopped her painting and waited for more instructions. Not from Geppetto, but that damn cricket. She hadn't heard the little conscience in some time. But surely, since Geppetto had just said the new form of magic words — give it time — that meant her little bug was close by.

After three minutes, she heard nothing.

Another two, another five.

Nothing.

Odd. He was usually such a persistent wretch. Perhaps he was quiet now because it was *her* time. Whatever she was waiting for, she had to do it now. Come out now. Tell Geppetto the truth. She was really—

"Ah, yes." Geppetto smiled down at the bird's wing she'd shaped in her daydreaming. "Just right. Perfect, my boy."

Pinocchio shut her mouth up tight. She finalized the last bird Geppetto loved so much. Now done, Geppetto placed the birdhouse inside her new workstation. "A first step into your brand new life," he said with only a touch of sadness in his tone. "You will become a young man very soon."

"Hurrah," she said without feeling.

"Come. Let's have a celebratory dinner." Geppetto clapped her on the back again.

Since there was no little voice telling her anything any longer, she went. She ate the meal with difficult enjoyment, and then she went to bed and dreamed of sawing her own dick off with one of Geppetto many tools.

The next morning, when she sat down at her new workstation, the name PINOCCHIO was painted across in black and yellow letters. "Now you can make whatever you think is the most beautiful thing," Geppetto said with his hands on her shoulders. "But don't get too carried away."

Geppetto left her alone for most of the day. After staring at her name, and wondering if Patricia or Penelope would suit her better, she came up with an idea. By the time Geppetto returned, and brought her a bowl of dinner he'd made, she'd crafted the torso, arms, and legs of her new puppet.

"Are you making a child so soon?" Geppetto asked. "You promised me no cribs just--"

"It's a woman, not a child," she interrupted. "And so

far, it's just a body."

She withdrew some twine from the workstation drawers and threaded it along the hooks on the back of the torso. She did the same to the delicate legs and arms which also held hooks. When she strung the whole thing together, she made the wooden female body — though its breasts were the only real thing that gave it away as a girl — dance to an unheard tune.

Geppetto hummed along to give her a song. This small action — a tacit approval for her female longings — gave Pinocchio hope that one day, he'd understand. She opened her mouth to come out, once again, but that damn conscience returned.

"Give it time," the voice said.

"Ugh. I thought it was time? Isn't that what you've been telling me this whole time? You'd think I'd be late by now."

"No, no." Geppetto tapped her shoulder and pointed to her dinner. "I brought it out for you. Don't worry about keeping an old man company. You clearly know what you're doing."

"No, I don't."

"This puppet is just like the one I made," Geppetto said, his voice proud and deeply nostalgic. "You are leaps and bounds of where I expected you to be at this age. You're turning into a fine young man and—"

"I'm not!"

"You are. I know you've had a hard start, a difficult beginning, and that Lampwick--"

"Geppetto!" Pinocchio snapped. She placed her hands on the side of her father's arms and gripped him hard to keep his attention. When his dark eyes widened, and it was clear she had his eternal focus, she almost baulked. She was a blank slate, worse than her mind as a puppet: she was devoid of all desire and embodiment for several seconds.

Then something snapped. It sounded like a piece of dried wood caught in a fire. And she felt everything again. Her body. Her pain. Her lack of a proper role in the world. Lies, all lies, and though her nose didn't grow any longer, there was a pressure there that would not relent. She wasn't just a former puppet; she was trapped in a cage of a biological body that would decay much faster and leave a far deeper mark on her soul than any simple fable. It was the wrong body, and she couldn't even tell the man who had made her. She wanted so much — too much — and now she was ready to trade everything for the truth.

"I'm not who you think I am," she finally said. "I'm not your son."

"Dear Pinocchio...." Her father touched her cheek. She looked away. Her nose itched, but it did not grow. She felt her father's sadness and heard it in his sighing, but she couldn't meet his gaze again. "You'll always be my son."

"I'd rather be your daughter."

"What?"

She bit her lip. *Now or never.* She waited a split second for her conscience to kick in and tell her to wait. But there was nothing, only her own breath, only her truth. She was happy to fill up the empty air with her confession. "I'm a girl. I should have been a girl. I want breasts like this. I want arms and legs like this. And I want to dance like this."

She pulled the strings of the puppet. Without a head, it was rather garish to watch it move — but this absence only gave Pinocchio more inspiration. She held the puppet body below her own neck. She mimicked its dance as she made it dance. The wooden body knocked together and sounded like the patter of rain. She tricked herself, for a minor moment, that this was her form. That her feet kicked high into the air as her arms swayed, and she was all woman as she did all of this.

But I'm not. And never will be.

Pinocchio crumbled onto the floor of the workroom, tears staining her face. Sawdust stuck to her cheeks. She breathed in more pine dust and shavings. She coughed. She held her doll-body close to her and begged and begged for the exchange.

"I want to be a woman!" she wailed. "I wish it, I create it, I ask for it — but it never happens. I've made this puppet, but it won't change me. I need you, Geppetto. I need you to make it so."

The room was quiet. Not even Pinocchio's heart or breathing seemed to make a sound. She wondered if she'd gone backwards in time, and now she was all wooden limbs and strings like before she'd been made real.

"My dear," Geppetto voice broke the silence. He crouched down with a crack of his knees; he crunched over some of the wood chips to scoot closer to her; and his breath quivered in his lungs as he also inhaled the detritus of the workspace. "My dear child."

Pinocchio felt a hand on her back. She didn't dare meet her father's eyes. She didn't dare do anything but stare at her feet, her boy-feet clad in brown shoes, and let all her tears flow down. Soon, Geppetto moved his hand up and down rhythmically. He hummed the same tune as before and nudged her shoulders. He plucked at her back as if she had strings.

"I'm not your puppet, Papa," she said. "I'm sorry."

"Nonsense. You were never supposed to be my puppet."

"I'm not your son, either. I'm—"

"My child," he said. "And my child you'll always be."

"Child?" Pinocchio raised her face. She scratched herself on a woodchip as she brushed away tears. She thought she heard acceptance in Geppetto's voice. She thought she heard love and kindness. She saw the same feelings in his eyes, within the wrinkles of his skin, and inside his worn-down hands that now held her female wooden body. Love. Acceptance. Pride. Truth, sweet and glorious truth.

Geppetto extended the female puppet out to her. "Let's call the fairy. Maybe we can make another wish and give you all you want."

Pinocchio wrapped her arms around her father, so much tighter than all the other times before. She clung to him, she sobbed into his shirt, and she otherwise melted into him. When she pulled away, she half-expected to be already changed. For her body to become like soft wood all over again, and for the changes she desired to be whittled down in some places and built up in others.

But she was the same. A boy's body, through and through.

She was also more than the wood that had made her, too. She was oak and pine and mahogany; she was Geppetto child, and she always would be. She was also herself, a single person, and this time, her body would be one that she'd made herself for herself. Her body would be alive with wonder, magic, and hope.

"Just one more thing," she said, grasping her father's

hands. "Let me make the head for the doll, too. I want different hair."

By the time the blue light of early dawn faded into orange, the entire female puppet was done. She wore a gingham dress with a pink and blue checkered shirt underneath. Her blonde hair was in braids down past her shoulders, tied off with blue ribbons. She wore clogs, and when Pinocchio pulled her puppet strings, she danced a merry jig to the same tune Geppetto hummed.

"Is it time?" Geppetto asked. "Let me know when I can call the fairy."

Pinocchio waited for one minute. She felt nothing tugging against her ear to listen. No words of wisdom or warning, nothing holding her back.

It was time now for everything she ever wanted.

Pinocchio nodded to her father. He called out for the Blue Fairy, completing the same incantation and magical ritual that he'd done to conjure her and make his son.

For a while, everything was the same. Pinocchio's chest tightened and worry spread over her skin in goose bumps. She was about to ask her father — *why on earth do humans call this goose bumps?* — when something glimmered on the horizon. The colour of the sky changed as the glow of the Blue Fairy made herself known. She was still several miles away, but she was coming.

"I think that's her," Geppetto said. He squeezed his daughter's hand. "She'll know what to do."

"She will," Pinocchio said, and squeezed Geppetto's hand in return. "And then I think my luck will change."

Lena Ng

Lena Ng lives in Toronto, Canada. Her short stories have appeared in eighty publications including Amazing Stories and Flame Tree's Asian Ghost Stories and Weird Horror Stories. Her stories have been performed for podcasts such as *Gallery of Curiosities, Utopia Science Fiction, Love Letters to Poe,* and *Horrifying Tales of Wonder.*

She has a short story collection titled *Under an Autumn Moon.*

Lena brings with her her story 'Rumperella.'

Rumperella

Once upon a time, there lived a little man named Rumpelstiltskin who had descended from imps and who therefore could perform small magic such as transforming straw into gold. Although he had no want for a wife, since he found women generally irksome, he had a desire for a son, to whom he would pass down his secret magical skills, simple as they were, and who would take care of him in his dotage.

So over the years, he tried cajoling women into giving up their children for straw-spun gold. These women had many children, and since they lived in poverty, they would be comforted into thinking they were procuring a better future for the child by giving him or her away.

With glee, Rumpelstiltskin took home his first child, wrapped in swaddling, who was hastily thrust into his arms. But — egads! — as he unwrapped the swaddling, he discovered it was a girl. He gnashed his teeth in disappointment and quickly went about finding another, making sure this time the child was a boy. But with some thought, he realized there were uses for a girl for domestic duties: cooking, cleaning, mending clothes, weeding the garden, and tending to the chickens and the like. He named her Rumperella and his new son Rumpelstiltskin, Jr — for clarity's sake to be referred to as Junior — and carefully brought them up as he had envisioned.

To the boy, he taught reading and writing, and his magic of spinning straw into gold. As Rumperella swept the floor, and afterward, sliced the potatoes, she looked on with longing as Rumpelstiltskin taught Junior to twist the straw, say the words, and spin the wheel until the dull straw burnished to brightness. She put the potatoes into the pot and asked, "May I try now?"

"No," said Rumpelstiltskin as he patted smug Junior on the head. "No girls allowed."

The boy became an echo of his father and agreed, "Yeah, Rumperella. No girls allowed."

Although Rumperella was not treated unkindly, she felt stuck in a box. Every time she wanted to learn something, not only to spin straw into gold, but also to speak to birds and coax them into doing her bidding — another small magic — she was told to pluck a chicken, or start the fire, or wash the socks. To get around this, as she did the chores, she would position herself beneath a window or near a door or by the hearth, to eavesdrop on these lessons and she would practice in secret.

Over the years, Rumperella grew into a young woman, but a homely one at that. She was as plain as the day was long, with big front teeth like a rabbit, small gopher-like eyes, and a figure shaped by a diet of stew, since her father was a meat-and-potatoes man. Although Rumperella had never met her, her natural mother wasn't a pretty one, and there was nothing to brag about with her father who had the long, hairy face of a goat.

One morning, as Rumperella was collecting the eggs, she heard the blare of a trumpet. Since she had secretly learned to enchant the birds, this was her quickest chore and it was done in a blink. She set the basket of eggs down on the floor of the coop and rushed out to investigate the cause of the excitement.

"Here ye, here ye!" said the lanky messenger, liveried in green and yellow, while standing on a crate in the middle of the village square. "Prince Charming is proud to announce the date of the Damsels Ball. In seven nights' time, all young, unattached ladies are invited to meet the prince and have a chance at becoming his bride."

The village gathering was all atwitter. With the small crowd of customers, the cabbage seller quickly sold out. Prince Charming, their darling, handsome prince, was looking to be wed. Who would that special girl be?

Rumperella went home and looked at her basket of eggs. She looked at the clothes hanging on the line and the weeds that had to be picked. She thought — wait for it — what if *she* went to the ball? What if *she* was picked by Prince Charming? Picked like a flower from this garden of weeds. This could be her ticket out of there, to be more than a maid to her father and brother. Rescued from her downtrodden fate.

That afternoon, Rumperella hummed as she folded the clothes. She muttered her imaginary plans as she gathered the straw. Rumpelstiltskin was getting annoyed. As Rumperella was growing older, she was growing more irksome.

"What's all this nonsense about?" he asked as Rumperella flitted about the floor in an inelegant semblance of

Fairy Tales from the Rock

a waltz. She grabbed hold of Junior and spun him around, interrupting his alchemy lesson.

"I'm practicing," Rumperella replied, "for the ball."

Rumpelstiltskin laughed long and loud. "Princes don't marry gophers."

"He might marry this one."

Rumpelstiltskin was too amused to forbid it.

At the ball, Rumperella smiled as prettily as she could at Prince Charming, which revealed her rabbity teeth, while she fluttered her gopher-ish eyes. She wore clothes she herself had sewn from loose threads of spun gold she had swept from the floor, and she definitely felt like a princess. The Prince, resplendent in a white military uniform with gold braid trim on blue lapels, instinctively flinched. He didn't bother to acknowledge her presence let alone turn on the charm, and stalked off in another direction.

But Rumperella was not so easily deterred. This was the man who could rescue her from drudgery. If she married another peasant, it would be the same life as with her father. She followed him around the ballroom, and as he turned to greet damsel after damsel, hovering nearby was that carrot-crunching smile.

But just as Rumperella had weaseled her way into the Prince's company once again, the Prince's eyes suddenly lit up. She followed his gaze and found the object of his attraction. A girl whose hair was as bright as spun gold, who was clothed in a gossamer blue gown as though by a fairy godmother, and whose delicate feet wore equally delicate slippers of glass.

Rumperella's heart sank. She knew now there was no hope. What could *she* offer if she had no beauty? Envy of this girl's beauty along with her chance at a new life dug a dagger deep into Rumperella's heart. It slowly mineralized into stone.

Soon after the clock struck midnight, the girl in the glass slippers fled, likely having missed curfew, leaving one of the slippers behind on the stairs, and the party was disbanded.

Rumperella plodded back home. Both her father and brother were asleep and thus couldn't make fun of her. The next day, she continued her chores as usual, but more quietly, more subdued, and so on the next day and the next. Her father and brother didn't notice as long as the eggs were collected, the chickens were plucked, and meals were hot on the table.

The girl, it was discovered, was named Cinderella, a girl with an upbringing much like Rumperella's own, who was forced to play maid to the family and whose fairy godmother taught her to speak to the birds. The Prince was enchanted enough to wed right away. On the day of the wedding, there was a huge, kingdom-wide party. Rumperella decided to stay home. Her lost chance still gnawed at her heart.

Sometimes, she would haunt the perimeter of the castle, wondering how happy Princess Cinderella's life was now, married to a handsome prince. How lucky she was to be picked like a flower. But one day, she heard some strange sounds, like those of someone weeping. She looked up and saw the new princess, leaning from a turret window, weeping to wake the dead.

Rumperella looked about and coaxed a nearby bird

Fairy Tales from the Rock   211

from a tree. "Find out what's wrong," she said, and it flew up to the turret. The bird and the princess conversed for some time before it returned to Rumperella's shoulder. It relayed the princess's tale.

In their heady honeymoon days, she and the Prince were very happy. But a wedding is only the start of the hard labour of marriage. It wasn't long before the magic of Cinderella's looks wore off, and since Cinderella grew up poor and uneducated, she could not converse of jewels or art or books, nor make witty conversation, and knew nothing of etiquette or horses. She couldn't laugh at his jokes, such as they were, since she couldn't understand them, and the Prince grew bored of her beauty.

Instead, the Prince rediscovered his love for gold, since he had massive debts for fancy clothes and other sundries, and became bitter at his bride's lack of wealth. He had even threatened to find some reason to cut off her head, so he could marry a bride of means.

Rumperella felt sorry for the princess, but even more sorry for herself. Here, this beautiful princess surrounded by privilege was complaining about her problems while Rumperella was so homely, she could never be married nor have a child, which now as a grown woman she longed for, let alone be a princess. She disguised herself as a servant, and armed with clean linens, made her way to Princess Cinderella's turret.

Cinderella was crying and crying, and her nose was red and runny. Rumperella began making the bed. She picked up some of the clothes off the floor, and when she was close enough to whisper under her breath, she said, "I heard you have money problems."

Cinderella lifted her head from the dressing room table and wiped her nose with the back of her hand. "Where did you hear that?" she asked with a hiccup.

"A little bird told me." Rumperella placed the wrinkled skirts and undergarments into a hamper. "Tell the prince that you can spin straw into gold and all your money troubles will be over."

"You'd do this for me?" Since Cinderella already had a fairy godmother, she took this turn of events in stride.

A malicious glitter twinkled in Rumperella's eyes and she said, "Of course." Even though she had never actually transformed the straw directly, there was always a first time.

Cinderella was sitting on a straw bale in the dungeon when Rumperella appeared. "Okay," she said with chipper note in her voice. "Let's get started."

Rumperella gave a sharkish smile that made her long teeth look even longer. "Let's not be hasty. We haven't yet discussed a price."

Cinderella was taken aback. "What? What do you mean?" The colour drained from her face. "When I first told the prince, he laughed. Then he said it was impossible. Then he said if I don't have a room full of gold in the morning, it'll be off with my head." She looked a bit green. "We can split the gold if you want."

Rumperella's expression looked as stony as her heart. "I don't want gold. I want something more precious, something I've longed for. Your firstborn child."

Cinderella burst into hysterics and was making such a racket that Rumperella came up with a quick suggestion that would give her some hope. "I'll give you a chance though. If, on the day I return, you can say my name within three guesses, I'll leave you the child."

Cinderella whimpered and nodded, and Rumperella turned the dungeon into shining gold. The prince stood in shock the next morning and thought how lucky he was to have both a beautiful *and* wealthy wife. The rest of her flaws seemed to have been forgotten.

Nine months later, Cinderella gave birth, and Rumperella came to collect. Although Rumperella's name resembled her own, Cinderella could not guess the name. "Babbitty Rabbitty?" she guessed. "Hyzenthlay? Bunnicula?" Cinderella believed strongly in the power of intuition, but in this case, it let her down.

Nope, nope, and nope, and Rumperella left with the child.

The baby slept in a basinet in Rumperella's room like a plump, little angel. She had explained to her father and brother that she had found the baby in the rushes. Junior, having finished his studies, left for adventures and mischief throughout the kingdom, leaving Rumpelstiltskin without a companion or a pupil.

As Rumpelstiltskin grew more lonely, he started to see Rumperella as less irksome. Magnanimously, he decided to teach her his magic of spinning straw into gold. Since he didn't know she had eavesdropped on their lessons, he thought she was a quick study.

As she grew in love for the child, Rumperella's stone heart demineralized and returned to flesh and blood. With this new heart, she knew could not deprive the baby of knowing his true mother, just as she had been deprived of knowing her own. She bundled the babe in beautiful, well-crafted clothes and gently placed him a basket. She returned him to the palace's door with a note and a gift of a lucky jewel as a reminder of one who loved him enough to return him. The princess and the prince wept with joy at the return of their child, and were generous enough to announce their forgiveness of her act, and in fact, made her his godmother.

Rumperella thought about how good she felt by doing good acts. She didn't need a Prince Charming to rescue her from a life of drudgery; she could rescue herself from her fate. She wouldn't be picked like a flower, but didn't picked flowers wilt? She spun straw into gold thread, made beautiful clothes, and sold them to both villagers and royalty alike. She also used the gold to buy food for the poor and to build cottages for the elderly or feeble, but only in secret, since she knew that man's greed for gold would cause her no end of grief. No other woman had to give up her child for money.

Although she was still homely, the gentleness and generosity of Rumperella's new heart shone through her face and she looked, if not beautiful, then appealing. Her smile made others feel good about themselves and lit up their hearts like stars. One day, after she had visited a widow with five children, bringing her a basket bursting with bread, fruit, and cheese, she felt a small tug on her skirts.

A small, shy boy with rowdy black hair looked up at her in wonder. "Are you a princess?" he asked. "Princess Charming?"

A princess? Her? Rumperella's face transformed into something truly beautiful as she slowly nodded yes. And she lived happily ever after.

David James Lynch

David James Lynch is an award-winning author who has spent the last two decades working as an educator and school counsellor.

He grew up in the small town of Bellevue Beach, and currently lives in Paradise, Newfoundland and Labrador with his wife Tara, and their children, Norah and James.

His short fiction won both the 2022 and 2021 WritersNL Nightmare Writing Contests.

He has a habit of purchasing more books than he'll ever be able to read, believing a home always has room for one more bookcase.

In May 2023 he released the first novel in his epic fantasy series, *All Things Broken*.

Poultice

"Is it true, Grandfather?"

The young girl speaks in little more than a whisper, though there are none for miles in the meadows and marshes through which they now tread. She stops, and turns to face him fully, her eyes narrow. "Did you really meet *William?*"

The old man, bent low and reaching for a particularly plump golden-orange berry, slows in his task. His fingers hesitate, then pick the berry and place it in his wooden pail. Half full, he notes. He stands, twisting to stretch his aching muscles; one hand rubbing his knuckles against his lower back, the other holding the pail.

"Molly," he says gently. "Have you been listening to tales?"

The girl smiles. Tall for her twelve years, she prefers kneeling to pick berries. She looks at him now, one knee on the ground, a pail of her own resting on the other. She stops, and rests both arms on the rim of her berry bucket.

"I've always been told," she says, "to be mindful. Observant. Unless in the forest, of course. Then, I must be *watchful and wary*." She says these last three words in a deep, gruff voice, imitating that of her grandfather. The old man smiles, impressed as ever by the girl's ability to replicate him. His smile is genuine, but falters as he looks over the girl's head at the copse of trees in the distance. He has no fear of the forest, but the girl's question has replaced his light mood with one of unease.

"I wasn't *trying* to listen in on the conversation," she continues, following his gaze. "I heard Mother and Father speaking a few days ago." Her voice goes quiet. "It was Uncle Daniel's birthday. He'd have been forty. Mother was upset. They got to talking and... I was outside, weeding the garden beside the window. I... I didn't mean to listen in. I was going to leave, but—" She shrugs. "Flower beds won't weed themselves."

He narrows his eyes, tilts his head slightly to the side.

"Yes, I know, but... they spoke of his disappearance. Him and that woman. Father tried to console Mother; told her she shouldn't lose hope. It's only been a few months, and Uncle Daniel has always been... unpredictable. They could return." She waits until their eyes meet. "They said *you* returned. That time."

Ah yes, he thinks. *That* time. Still he doesn't speak, allowing her to share what she will.

"I've heard bits and pieces over the years," Molly says. "Haven't really been able to piece it all together. Stuff said by old fishermen on the wharf who hush up when they notice me. But, Grandfather, I'm *twelve* years old. Almost thirteen. Don't you think it's time I've been told the truth?"

The old man smiles inwardly. *Twelve* — said as if she'd reached a wise old age at which all of life's secrets should be shared with her, for certainly she would understand. After all, she's *twelve* years old.

"I know what you're thinking," she says. "You're thinking I'm still a child. You're thinking I'm not ready to hear the story you'd tell." She pauses. "Or maybe, you think I won't believe you…"

Closer to the mark, he thinks. He takes a few steps, and lowers himself to sit on a fallen tree at the edge of the marsh, a snag that had finally given way to the relentless nor'easters that pound the coast.

"So…" He adjusts himself and pats the log beside him. Molly sits, careful to secure her pail on the soft ground. The old man looks in the bucket. "Do you know why they're called bakeapples?"

"It's because—" Molly stops. Her brow furrows. The old man smiles, seeing that she was sure she knew the answer before she even considered *whether* she knew it, because, well… *twelve*. She shakes her head.

He folds his arms over his knees. "Some say there was a French traveler, years ago, visiting an area much like this." He gestures to the marsh. "The Frenchman noted the berries, and wondered what variety they might be. The French word for berry is *baie*. He asked his companions what the berry was called. *Baie qu'appelle?*"

Molly watches him. Her lips purse beneath a look of confusion.

"Baie qu'appelle," he says again, more slowly this time.

She mouths the words, thinks, then chortles as the meaning strikes her. "Funny."

"What's *funny*, child, is that the answer to the question is the question itself."

Fairy Tales from the Rock

"That's quite deep, Grandfather." A smirk.

"Of course, we could just call them cloudberries, as do some regions."

"Is there a region where they're referred to as 'change-the-subject-berries'?"

"And now it's you who's funny, little one." He stops then as the moniker triggers a memory in him, and his face changes.

Molly, of course, notices this. "Grandfather?"

"Just… just a memory, dear." He takes a slow breath as he rights himself, and pats his granddaughter on the hand. A swallow sings in the distance, but its song is lost in the cries of the seagulls.

"There's no easy answer to your question. Like the bakeapple, sometimes the answer simply raises more questions." He absently rubs the callused fingers of his right hand. "My memories are like berries, love; very few end up in the pail. But…" He sighs. "I'll share what I can gather."

Molly sits up quickly. Her grandfather raises a finger in gentle warning. "Recollections are *fallible*, Molly. Remember that. They're thoughts in a heavy rolling mist, in a forest that sleeps uneasily. And in such circumstances, many things might be lost…"

Sam Greene felt certain that he'd be the next child stolen.

In the months since the dozen or so families had settled themselves in the area now referred to as Fair Ridge, three children had disappeared.

Only two had returned.

The tiny community had settled in the location due mainly to its proximity to the bountiful fishing ground that lay nearby. Simple dwellings had been erected, and it was hoped that the surrounding land would support the modest gardens of root vegetables required for a hamlet so small.

The first growing season showed promise, and the women and youth worked diligently to tend the fields while the men harvested what they could from the cold, rough sea. Wells had been dug, but the main source of fresh water was the river flowing at the community's periphery. The work was hard, and even the little ones found themselves spending several hours each day engaged in necessary chores.

Sam hauled water.

It was an arduous task, but one in which he found satisfaction. When he'd first begun hauling, the older women had ruffled his hair and told him that his water made the very best tea, and he'd beamed. He'd work all the harder, and brought more water from the river than any of his peers.

But presently, smiles and laughter were as scarce as fatback pork. The happiness that usually permeated the privations of life on Fair Ridge was all but gone. Three children, on three separate occasions, had gone missing. The first, seven-year-old Sally Blackmore, had disappeared one misty morning as she picked berries. The townsfolk had searched the area through wind, rain, and despair. *She'll surely catch her death in this weather*, some whispered. Her mother Catherine was inconsolable. Through stifled sobs and muttered prayers, she maintained her certainty that the girl would be returned to her. And so, she was. During a break in the early morning rain, Sally emerged from the woods.

Cries of elation met the girl. Catherine fell to her knees, embracing Sally in a vice-like grip. She held her daughter for some time, refusing to let her go even as the wet ground soaked through the hem of her dress. As she felt the chill of the earth beneath her, a chill of another sort shot along the length of her arms.

She released the girl and leaned back, her face tightening with confusion. She reached out, and smoothed the girl's dress, its floral pattern cheerful against the overcast day. The dress was clean. And it was dry.

"Sally?" Catherine's voice cracked, though she worked to present a calm exterior. "Sally, love... Where *were* you?"

The child smiled. She looked behind her, as if the answer might be found there. Her smile faltered a little, but not completely.

"I... I was dancing. It was lovely. They like to dance."

Catherine was on her feet instantly. "Who, child?" She took hold of Sally. "Where were you? Who were you with?"

Several of the townsfolk looked at each other warily. The closest women fidgeted, wringing their hands in their dirty aprons.

"I... I can't remember." There was no fear on Sally's face. "Why are you so upset, Mother?"

"Why am I upset? *Child!* We thought we'd lost you!"

"But... I was only gone a couple of hours."

Silence fell over the group. Again, looks were exchanged. Catherine turned to the others, seeking answers, but there were none to be found.

Sally had been missing for four days.

Georgie Doyle disappeared under similar circumstances. One moment, he'd been collecting wood for the fire, and the next, he simply wasn't there.

Only two days passed before Georgie returned. He walked out of the trees, his arms laden with wood and a look of small concern on his face.

The fuss of the reunion was similar to that seen when Sally returned. Georgie was several years older than Sally, but a child still. The worry that wracked his family and friends was no different than that experienced for the girl. But Georgie remembered more than Sally. Whether this was due to his being older, or the lesser number of days spent missing, none could know. What they did know was that his words were indeed a cause for concern.

"He's not happy we're here," Georgie said quietly.

Georgie's father, Alexander, a stern, no-nonsense type of fellow, removed Georgie from his mother's embrace. "Who?" He grabbed his son's arm in a tight grip. "Who, boy?"

Georgie seemed not to notice the muscular hand wrapped around his shoulder. His eyes were fixed on the forest.

"He said we settled…" Georgie struggled to remember. "…in a most *unfortunate* location. We have to move."

The townsfolk began to mumble amongst themselves,

speculating on who might be responsible for the disappearances. The hushed voices faded after several moments and they turned back to Georgie. *What did he look like?* they asked. *Did he tell you his name? Was he alone?* Their faces grew serious. *Did he hurt you?*

Georgie looked up. There was confusion on his face, but it didn't appear to be caused by the questioning. Indeed, he seemed to have a distant look since he'd emerged from the forest; the look of a person perplexed by a riddle whose answer should be entirely obvious.

"He…" Georgie seemed to search for words as if looking for ripe berries. "He said… we're on his *path.*" He looked around, at the dwellings the folk had built with such pride. "We… we built on his path. He said we have to move. Said the next child that was lost would be kept. He…" Georgie shivered suddenly. He looked down at his bare arms, and the hair standing on end. *Goosepimples*, his father often called them with a serious face. *Someone must have walked over my grave.* His mother dismissed such notions. She'd usually rub the bumps on her own arms away with a smile. *Just a case of the willies,* she'd say.

Georgie's head jerked up, and he looked into the worried eyes of his father. *"Will,"* he said. He made a futile effort to rub away the chills that covered his arms. "The little ones called him *The Will*…"

The third child to disappear was Anna McCarthy.
Anna McCarthy was kept.

In the weeks since little Anna had been lost, the dark cloud of despair hung over Fair Ridge. Sam watched as the townsfolk quietly went about their business, completing their chores with mechanical movements. Smiles were essentially non-existent. Anna's family, though they continued to search diligently, seemed to be losing hope. Some began to suggest that they actually consider moving the village, which led to an emotional discourse. *Where would we move?* they asked. *How far away would be deemed a safe distance from this supposed path? Where is this path anyway? There was no path when we cleared this area!*

Others took a different approach. *We can't let a madman determine our fate. This must be the work of someone entirely deranged. Someone wronged in the past, possibly with a grudge against a Fair Ridge resident. We'll be lucky if he doesn't set Fair Ridge aflame!*

Georgie, to one side, looked up suddenly. "He had a flame," the boy said.

Those gathered turned to Georgie — the closest, Syl Byrne, went to his knee. "What'd you say, boy?"

"Will. The Will. He had a flame. I... I remember following it." His eyes got a little wider. "I *followed* it. Through the trees. It was dark. There were lots of birds singing. It was... musical. And I followed the flame. I remember the flame, the way it danced. It led me." He seemed surprised at how much he now remembered. "I stopped in a... it was like a circle. Or a ring." He smiled, lost in memory. "A ring of mushrooms."

It was likely that some of the townsfolk had considered the possibility; couples whispering suspicions in the witching hour of sleepless nights. But none had spoken the thought in public. None, until Syl Byrne turned to his neighbors, his voice full of resignation and dread.

"It's the fairies."

Fairy Tales from the Rock

In the days that followed, the search continued, though the despair and anger were now tinged with fear.

Fairies.

None were prepared for this turn of events. Madmen, however evil, could be reckoned with — understood, to an extent. But these unknown creatures were another matter entirely. The rudimentary weapons the townsfolk carried on their searches would likely be useless, if in fact they were even able to find the elusive fae. Sam listened to the adults as they spoke, sharing what little lore they know. *Could the fairies be seen with the human eye? Yes, the young ones had seen them, but what if the creatures didn't want to be seen? Were they benevolent, or the malicious sort? Obviously the latter, as they'd taken children. But no harm had come to Sally or Georgie. There was still hope for Anna. Was there a limit to the length of her capture? Was this the final ultimatum? Leave, or lose your children? Would she be returned if they did so?*

None could know.

They continued to search, putting off the inevitable decision they knew they would have to make sooner rather than later.

And then, the land turned.

It began with the potatoes. The crop had been promising; the plants breaking through the ground early. The leaves grew larger, their colour deep and healthy, until one day, they suddenly began to falter. Despite favorable conditions, the leaves withered, the plants drooping with a sadness that reflected that of the people. No intervention could revive them. And then, on a beautiful July morning, the sun rose to reveal gardens full of terrible intruders.

Thistle, as if magically grown, had appeared overnight. Interspersed with the thistle were nettles and hogweed that eagerly filled the spaces between the vegetable plants. The villagers worked to remove the invasive plants, but their efforts were futile. Each day the rising sun revealed fields overrun with weeds that had reaffirmed their position throughout the night.

As the residents struggled to deal with loss of their crops, a new challenge afflicted thevvillage. Sam heard several of the adults commenting on the drinking water, noting how it was decidedly *off*, as if a generous pinch of salt had been added. Jeb Walsh, one of the village's bigger residents, turned toward the young ones that were nearby, his fists clenched. His low voice rumbled slowly, quietly from his throat.

"If one of ye thinks this is a time for pranks and tomfoolery, I'll teach ye the difference."

"Jeb!" his wife said, smacking his arm. "Leave off the young ones. Look at the scare you've given 'em. Love of God, you got young Sally crying."

"Brackish," said Alexander Doyle. He spit the water into the dirt. "This wasn't the young ones." He paused, took a breath. "But I'd bet Grandfather's old stopwatch there's *little ones* to blame…"

"Father? Where are you going?"

Sam watched as his father hurried about behind the house, shoving supplies in his sack.

"Upriver a bit." Alphonsus Greene turned to his son. "I don't believe in watching wounds fester, Son. Right now, Fair Ridge is festering. Only a fool turns his back on a chance to heal."

Sam thought a pained look crept across his father's face as he spoke. "I'm going to go up the river, see if I can find the source of the problem. Barring that, I'll see if I can't find another source of good water." He smiled thinly. "Best grab your jacket. You might need it."

Sam's eyes went wide. The children had, for the most part, been expressly forbidden to go into the forest. His father nodded. "We're not goin' too far, lad. It's a sunny day. I told your mother where we were headed." He smiled again, but to Sam's eye, it seemed a little forced. Alphonsus ruffled his son's hair. "I also have it on good authority that no one can haul water like young Sam Greene."

Sam beamed as he bustled about, readying his things. *What would Michael and Ronnie say,* Sam wondered, *when he told them that he'd been chosen for an excursion upriver? They'd be proper jealous, no doubt.*

Sam pulled on his jacket. Though it was July, there was an unseasonable chill in the air and a low fog hung over the land. Sam cared little. It was a glorious morning in his eyes. He saw the potential for a bit of excitement. He saw a break from the village, and the opportunity to boast to the other youngsters of how he helped the residents of Fair Ridge.

What young Sam Greene did not see, however, was the unfortunate reality that adults often have ulterior motives, and are sometimes called upon to make terribly difficult decisions.

The forest, for the most part, was quiet. There were few animals to be seen or heard, save the occasional bird that flitted about in the trees. Sam could hear the soft roar of Split River as they approached. It was a wide river, and while it was not at its most raucous at this time of year, its flow was still quite heavy. His father stopped occasionally, and carefully scooped water with a little tin cup. Each time, he'd taste it, spit it to one side, and shake his head.

They continued like this for some time. Sam assumed they must have traveled a mile or more by this point. If they did find good water, the lugging from this distance would be difficult indeed, even for a lugger like himself. But good water was important. The wells, the river and the pond, all likewise afflicted. *Tainted,* Catherine Blackmore said, *by those demons in the forest.* Several townsfolk shushed her when she spoke this way, but she still wasn't over Sally's ordeal and she maintained that she'd call them what she bloody well pleased, whether they could hear her or not.

Sam stopped suddenly when he noticed that Aphonsus was no longer walking. He looked back at his father, who gave a weak smile as he put a hand to his stomach. "Breakfast isn't agreeing with me, lad. Give me a couple moments in the alders, alright? Won't be long."

Sam nodded, showing no great deal of concern. It was a lovely morning, and the song of the river had a relaxing effect. He watched as his father stepped into the forest brush, branches cracking and rustling as he went. It went on for some moments, until the sound of the river covered his father's movement. Odd, Sam thought, for his father to want that much privacy. He shrugged inwardly, watching the river.

He thought he saw a rabbit dart in the underbrush at one point, but couldn't be certain. He looked across the river. It was fairly wide, perhaps thirty feet at some points, and in areas with rocks, a white froth was mixed and tossed about.

He looked back in the direction of his father. Still no sign. He took a couple of steps in that direction, leaning a little to look around a few thick spruce trees. Nothing. He turned again, and found himself face to face with the fairy.

His breath caught, and he froze. He quickly saw that there were two of the creatures: an older one, female, and a young male who stood just behind her.

"Sláinte," rasped the taller of the two. She looked much the same as a short woman, if not a little more ragged. The feet and hands of both fairies seemed disproportionately large to Sam; their noses a little longer than seemed natural, and their posture slightly hunched, as if from perpetually sneaking up on prey.

Prey like me, thought Sam.

"Please. Please don't..." was all Sam could manage. The closest fairy stepped forward.

"Master Will has asked us to—" But she wasn't afforded the chance to finish. From the bushes, Alphonsus Greene burst with extended hands and a roar that drowned out the river. Sam screamed as the chaos unfolded. He fell to the ground as his father flew over him, reaching for the fairies that, with incredible speed, had spun to run from the enraged man. But Alphonsus had the element of surprise in his favor and was able to grab the startled, older fairy as she ran along the riverbank. She cried out, not so much in pain, but in fear and confusion. The small fairy ahead of them stopped. When Alphonsus — still gripping the older fairy — lunged for the younger one, the small creature twisted away. As it took a step backwards, the soft earth of the riverbank gave way, and the fairy plunged into the water below.

The fairy that Alphonsus held — and now assumed to be the mother — thrashed and screamed with an intensity that matched that of the fairy in the water. So shocking it was that Alphonsus released his grip on the creature, almost falling back as he did so. Beside them, Sam's screams joined the chorus.

The fairy on the bank began running alongside the one in the water. Alphonsus followed, with Sam close behind. The small fairy had been pulled into the current, and while it was not particularly forceful, it was well beyond his ability to navigate.

"Can't... can't swim!" the mother cried as she watched her child tossed about. She ran, her eyes never leaving the small one. Sam prayed his father would not try to grab her again — such was her desperation that she'd likely rip him to pieces to free herself. Alphonsus, Sam saw, was confused; torn as to what he should do. He knew his father wanted to capture the creatures, to pull from them the whereabouts of Anna McCarthy. For the moment, they all just ran.

In the river, the fairy thrashed about, and managed to grab a small outcropping of rock that jutted from the waters. One hand slipped, and he slapped the other against the rock. The rock, Sam saw, was sharp, and while it provided a better grip than smooth stone, it must be dreadfully painful to hold, pulled as the creature was by the current.

The small company stopped on the riverbank. The fairy turned, tears in her eyes. She looked about desperately, seeking something to cling to, something to allow her to reach the child. Her head spun about crazily, fingers splayed and shaking.

Such pain, thought Sam. It was, in fact, quite similar to what he'd seen in the faces of Sally and Georgie's folk. The fairy was tortured; her face a visage of agony as she watched the youngling's thrashing limbs lose strength. Alphonsus must have seen all this as well, for before Sam could shout his protest, his father had removed his boots and sack, and jumped into the river.

Sam and the fairy screamed. The splash must have scared the youngling terribly, for it let go of the rock. A moment before he was pulled away by the current, Alphonsus' hand clamped around the fairy's slender wrist.

It took some work to get the creature back to the riverbank, but Sam knew his father was as strong as he was determined. A few minutes later, kicking savagely, he reached the bank, the fairy clinging desperately to his shirt, buttons ripped away. He grabbed an overhanging branch, and hoisted the young one to the waiting arms of his mother. She grabbed the child and stepped back several paces from the dangerous water. She fell to her knees, wrapping herself around the body of her child in the most tight, yet tender of embraces.

Sam grabbed his father's hand and gave what assistance he could as the man pulled himself up onto the bank.

None spoke.

After several minutes of gasping and reclaiming breath, the mother looked at the pair from Fair Ridge.

"You... saved him." Almost a question.

Alphonsus nodded. He stretched his pained neck and then focused his gaze on the fairy. "I did. And there is one that you might save as well."

The fairy was silent. She knew of whom Alphonsus spoke. Her eyes lowered as she spoke. "We... are Brounies." She must have seen that the word meant nothing to the pair. *"Brounies.* We... we have no authority. We serve the Will but—" She shook her head. "But he will not listen to us."

Alphonsus stood quickly, and the fairy raised a finger. To Sam's surprise, it stopped the man. "We... I can try," she continued. "I *will* try. But we are... *low* in his eyes." She held the child tighter. "I see what is in *your* eyes. The hatred. The fear. And I see that you are contemplating capture still. Ransom? A trade?" She shook her head sadly. "It will not work." Her voice lowered. "The only way to get the girl is to find the path. And only he... only The Will can open the path." A look of resignation crossed her face. "If you try to capture us, I will make it...difficult. But hear me, Master..." She paused.

"Greene," Alphonsus replied. "Alphonsus Greene."

She nodded. "Hear me, Master Greene. Let me *try* to convince The Will. It's the only hope for the girl. If you harm us — servants of The Will — you'll have more to fret about than troublesome weeds and water."

Sam could see that it was now his father's face that was tortured. He could try to capture the fairies, but he likely knew what it would bring about. Violent behavior, possibly torture at the hands of Anna's family. Vengeance from The Will. At that moment, Sam was glad he was a child, and such decisions were not his to make. Be that as it may, he spoke.

"Let them go, Father."

They all turned to the boy. He continued before he lost his courage. "I... I believe her. I think she will try." He looked into the forest, and thought of Anna. "We have to let her try."

The fairy stood, a hand still on the shoulder of the child. Sam noticed the blood that ran from the youngling's torn hands. His fingers hung limply, ravaged by the river rocks. "We owe you a debt," she said. "I owe you a debt, one that I will repay, however I can. *I promise.*" The youngling's head spun to his mother, who patted his shoulder to prevent him from speaking. "Do you understand the promise of a fairy, Master Greene?"

Alphonsus shook his head.

"*Fae* are unable to lie." She inclined her head toward the trees. Tentatively, she continued. "We will go now." She took a step, watching him all the while. "We will go... and we will keep our word."

After several long moments Alphonsus inclined his head, and the fae disappeared into the arms of the forest.

Days passed. Little changed in the village. The townsfolk struggled with their new reality, seeking solutions where there was none to be had. Each night, Sam could hear the hushed voices of his parents. The night of the encounter, Alphonsus had told his wife Beth about what had transpired. The voices had grown loud, then quieted again, and continued this way for many hours. There was a tension in the Greene house, but Beth must have understood her husband's reasoning, for she said nothing.

Several days later, Sam rose before the sun. He rushed for the chamber pot, his bladder painfully full. As he returned to his bed, he heard a noise — a rustling from without. Quietly, he moved to the window and squinted in the predawn light.

Heaven preserve us, he whispered.

He ran to the bedroom, roused his parents, and brought them to the back door. None spoke as they looked out on the yard.

Under the waning moon, a great pile of thorny weeds sat beside the potato garden. Within the stalks, two hunched creatures moved about. Weeds flew from their hands.

"It's them," Alphonsus whispered as he took a cautious step off the back porch. A board squeaked beneath his weight, and the figures in the garden froze. Alphonsus grimaced, and raised his hands as the figures turned toward the trees.

"Please," he hissed quietly. He took another step. "It's me. Alphonsus."

Slowly, the pair crept alongside the garden and approached the little family.

"We know," the older brounie replied. "We... are repaying the debt."

The fairies eyed Beth cautiously. Despite her shaking, her face was stoic. They now stood but several paces away.

"The Will?" Alphonsus asked.

"We are trying, Master Greene." She rubbed her shoulder. "Believe me."

Beth gasped suddenly, her hand flying to her mouth. The fairies started, ready to burst across the field. Beth took a slow step back, turned and rushed into the house, leaving the group in an awkward silence.

Sam watched the sky for long moments. The sun would soon rise, and the villagers would be about.

"Anna must be returned to us," said Alphonsus.

The fairy nodded sadly, wringing her hands in her tattered clothing. "I know that yo—" But she was cut off as Beth emerged from the dwelling. She held a large bowl and moved with purpose, but was careful not to startle them. She stopped at the top of the steps.

"The little one," she said quietly. There was pain on her face, Sam saw. "His hands. I need to see to that." The entire group turned to the youngling, who shoved his hands behind his back. Beth looked at the elder brounie. "This is your *child*, no?"

The brounie nodded.

"Then, as a mother, I know you'll appreciate that we cannot—" She paused for effect, pointing as only a mother points. "—*cannot* leave his hands in this dreadful state."

Sam was taken aback. He recalled the fear, the disbelief upon seeing these creatures. *Fairies*. It had taken him days to process what he'd seen and experienced. And here was his mother, speaking to the fae as if it were her own child. He watched and waited.

Slowly, the mother turned to the youngling. Something unseen passed between them, and she nodded. She took a step toward Beth and the youngling followed.

Beth sat on the bottom step, which seemed to lessen the fairies' apprehension. "Come," she said gently. "Folk will be about soon."

Ever so cautiously, the fairies approached the women. Their trust, Sam thought, was likely due to the fact that they knew Alphonsus depended on them to save Anna. As they'd said previously, to capture them would only serve to bring more misery to the village.

Beth worked quickly. Within the bowl, Sam saw that she had splashed milk over a bun of bread, along with leaves of some variety. Beth worked the combination into a paste, and tore the leaves into smaller bits. When she was happy with the consistency, she nodded to the youngling.

"It will help," Alphonsus said. "I *promise*, we'll help you."

The fairy gave another look to his mother, who nodded again. Sam wondered at his age. Was he as old as Sam? Much older? He was *fae*, after all. Whatever his age, the fairy was terrified. He extended his hands, and Beth gently covered the wounds with the gooey concoction.

Everyone started as the first cock crowed. The fairy, about to pull away, was held firm by Beth. "Just one more moment," she whispered. Lacking time, she ripped two strips of cloth from the bottom of her sleeping dress. With deft movement, she wrapped the youngling's hands and tied a gentle knot.

"Leave it as long as possible," she said to the mother.

The cock crowed again. "Now, go."

In moments, they were gone.

Sam and his father made an effort of weeding that morning, hoping to convince the village that they were up rather early and had done the work themselves. They went about their routines, completing chores, saying nothing of what had transpired.

Sam's thoughts raced throughout the day, and he saw to his tasks with slow effort. Late that afternoon, he returned home. He sat with a sigh on the back step, enjoying the quiet and the cool breeze that blew from the north. He rested his head against the railing, admiring the temporarily tidy potato garden as he ate a handful of bakeapples. He ate slowly, savoring each one as he burst them with the pressure of his tongue. When they were gone, he wiped his hands on the knees of his overalls and stood. He was turning toward the back door when movement caught his eye. He spun, narrow eyes watching the trees.

Slowly, he walked across the yard. He was sure that he'd seen something. He stopped, squinting. *There!* Just at the fringe of the trees. There was— *What in the blazes?*

The fairies! They'd returned but were not looking in his direction. They moved away from him, and... was the mother *carrying* the child? Sam felt his breath catch. Had the youngling's infection worsened so? Sam shook his head, panicked. He made to run after the pair, then stopped, turned and darted into the house. He cursed silently. His father had been gone since noon. His mother had spoken of picking berries with the other women. He looked about. There was no time.

Sam grabbed a bowl from the cupboard. Into it, he threw some bread, milk and... *Curses!* What was it Mother used? Oregano? Thyme? He recalled her joke, *There's never enough thyme,* she'd say.

Too true, he thought. He grabbed a sprig of the herb and dashed through the doorway, mixing the contents as he ran.

The evening sun sank as he ran to the trees. There was no sign of the fairies. He looked about, trying to recall where he'd last seen them. Settling on a copse of birch, he ran in that direction. He dismissed the sense of foreboding that arose in him and searched the area. In the distance, he thought he heard a branch crack underfoot. He raced toward the sound, realizing the foolishness of trying to run with a large clay bowl in his arms. Another crack, this time further away. He sighed and began shoving handfuls of the poultice into his overall pockets. Laying the bowl where he'd hopefully find it later, he began running.

Rays of sunlight shot through the canopy, speckling the forest floor with flecks of light. Sam stopped, listening hard for sound in the still woods. He was by no means a tracker. He'd need to rely on sound and—

He stopped. There was movement, far off in the shadows, as if a ray of light were being carried. He ran again, his eyes fixed on the light source. He ran between the trees, oblivious to distance and danger. He slowed, his legs tired. Funny, he thought. It seemed that when he slowed, the moving light slowed with him. *Waited* for him. He walked, the urgency lessening as he followed the light. It took him only moments to reach it.

A lantern, resting on a tree stump in the middle of a clearing.

A clearing ringed with mushrooms.

"Sláinte," the voice whispered from the shadows.

Beyond that point, things were hazy for Sam. He felt… tingly; lightheaded, as he assumed Syl Byrne felt after he'd imbibed in one too many, as was oft the case. He looked past the lantern, in the direction of the voice.

There was a figure in the shadows, barely discernible. Sam shook his head, thinking that he saw the horns of a stag rising over the sparkling eyes. But he felt no fear.

"I… think I'm lost."

"You're right where you ought to be, lad," said the voice.

To his left, he heard a soft giggle, and turned to see a young girl dancing toward him. He felt the urge to giggle as well. The air was thick with euphoria.

The girl approached him, skipping lightly.

"Care for a berry, Sam? They're *delicious*." Juice ran down her chin.

He smiled as he was offered the food. Strawberries, dipped in honey.

"Thank you, Anna."

She giggled again as he took them, and resumed dancing in slow circles, humming softly.

"You are welcome here," said the voice. *"As long as you wish."*

Sam looked around again, feeling the silly smile on his face. How long he stood this way he couldn't say. Minutes? Hours?

He was lost in the wonder of it all. Soft notes from a tin whistle wafted through the trees. Errant rays of sun still broke through the canopy, and fireflies appeared to float around him. *Yes,* he thought. *I could stay here.*

Anna giggled then, suddenly. "Sam Greene. Have you wet yourself?"

Surprised, he looked down to see the wet patch on the front of his overalls. He laughed then as he remembered.

"No," he smiled. "I… It's… it's just the poultice."

To the side, he saw the figure sit up.

"Come again," said the shadow.

"It's—" Sam reached into his pocket and retrieved a handful of the wet bread. "—just poultice… for the little one."

The figure was standing now, moving from beneath the trees. "So…" the voice was heavier. "'Twas you who assisted Bwachob?"

"Who ?"

"The brounie."

"Oh. Umm… yes. I helped… ah, Mother helped. Father promised we'd help, if they'd let us."

The figure didn't move. *"Promised… did he?"*

Sam nodded, toeing the mossy ground. "We don't believe in watching wounds fester."

The figure grunted. "The brounies," he said, "seem fond of promises also."

Time lapsed once more. Sam forgot the shadow. He danced with Anna. They ate fruits and berries. They sang. The rays of the sun took on the look of moonlight, and then sun once more.

They ate.

They danced.

They slept.

Sam awoke as the deep, rich voice spoke from behind the lantern.

"It's time to leave," the shadow said quietly.

The children's faces held a flat, still look. They did not express unhappiness. Nor was there joy. They simply waited.

"It's time," he repeated. He lifted the lantern from the stump and sighed. "Saved…by the *bread* in your pocket." He shook his head and began walking, muttering something about poultice and promises.

After a few moments he began to whistle a low, melancholy tune, and the enraptured children followed in his footsteps.

From the trees above, the brounies watched in silence.

Sam Greene stands with a groan.

It's been a long day, and now all he wishes for is the comfort of his rocking chair, a cup of tea, and a slice of his wife's freshly made bread.

Maybe a few berries to savor.

"So, that's it," he says. His eyes look deep into the forest. "Well… that's all I remember."

Molly stands and pulls him into the tightest hug. "Thanks, Grandfather."

Sam smiles through a grimace. "*Sweet Saint Michael*, love. I haven't been hugged like that since…"

And for a moment, he's back in Fair Ridge. Twelve

years old, embraced by his parents. Amidst the screams, the shouts and tears, he and Anna are pulled back into the fold. He's stammering, trying to explain, reaching into his pocket to show them the poultice he'd made; the reason he ran into the woods.

But there is no poultice.

Only breadcrumbs.

After eleven days and nights, it's completely dry.

They arrive back at Sam's little cottage just as the sun sets.

"Perfect timing," says Molly.

Sam smiles. "But never enough thyme."

Molly groans at the familiar joke as Sam leads her up the steps. He watches the sun's rays illuminate the field. "Come, child." His smile is unreadable. "This be the hour of The Will."

"The *Will?*" A voice from within. "The *Will O'The Wisp?*" Molly's grandmother emerges from the cottage, wiping her hands in her apron. She kisses Molly on the cheek, and points at Sam; points as only a wife can point. *"Samuel Greene,"* she smiles. "Have you been telling tales?"

Sam takes her hand in his own.

"Of course not, Anna." He kisses her hand, and winks at Molly. "Who'd believe me if I did?"

They enter the cottage, but not before Sam empties his pocket. He scoops out a handful of breadcrumbs and tosses it at the threshold of the doorway, leaving it to the night and what light it may contain.

W.H. Vigo

W.H. Vigo is a Jamaican-Canadian writer based in Toronto, Canada. They write horror and speculative fiction inspired by Caribbean folklore and their lived experience as an immigrant. In their daylight form, Vigo is a keen academic specializing in privacy and genetic surveillance (among other things the government doesn't want us to know about).

They also have a weakness for trashy reality TV and videos of baby animals.

They bring with them the short story 'Captured Land.'

Captured Land

Kingston, Jamaica 1965

Standing in silence next to an open grave, the guests stared at the place where a cream coloured casket leaned at its side like a seashell washed ashore. All that was heard was Pastor Boyce loudly finishing his prayers against a backdrop of whimpers and sobs. Across from the guests, outside of a home constructed from mausoleum bricks and tin sheets, was a woman named Nadine, and her young son Horace. The baby in Nadine's lap coughed terribly before it broke into a long cry.

"Talk-Straight, pass me one nappy off di clothes line for your sister," she asked.

"Yes Mama," her son answered, wiping grease from his forehead with the back of his arm.

Horace had acquired the nickname 'Talk-Straight' from the local merchants working at Kingston Port for his love of books and habitually speaking so-called 'proper' English, putting the foreign Whites at ease enough to open their wallets a little extra. At times, he would engage in conversation with customers, speaking on matters of philosophy and world history as the nauseating fumes from the polish scratched his throat and burned his nostrils. A tomato-faced jeweller from London once told him that he could've mistaken the boy for a scholar "if not for his age and complexion." While such comments aggravated him, survival was first and last on the agenda of each day. His earnings were just enough to buy the rice and chicken backs he cooked for dinner on their make-shift stove of cement blocks around a small pit fire.

"Here's the nappy for Daisy, Mama," Talk-Straight said, handing her the cloth and planting a kiss on the fussy baby's forehead.

Nadine promptly began changing the infant as the undertakers shovelled dirt into the pit.

"Boy...money make people do all kind of crazy tings," Nadine said, "Hear dats why di t'ieves killed poor Mr. Roy. Imagine! Kill one nice, likkle ol' man for him money," she shook her head. "People too heartless. Anyways, why you nah work tomorrow?"

Talk-Straight bit his lip and swallowed hard. His mother was illiterate and he didn't want to tell her how much the front page of the newspaper that day had scared him:

NINE STREET CHILDREN MISSING FROM KINGSTON HARBOUR. POLICE INVESTIGATING.

The streets had taught Talk-Straight that sometimes it was best to talk side-ways.

"Too many police. They say the port's overcrowded and I don't want to go out there and have them lock me up. Maybe next week things will calm down."

As the funeral guests dispersed, Talk-Straight looked over at the pastor, noticing his shiny, expensive shoes.

The pair locked eyes a moment and the stout holy man's face crinkled in disgust.

Maybe they'd find the children next week. If anyone cared to look.

Later that night, Talk-Straight sat up from his cardboard bed, sides aching. The legs of his small, snoring younger siblings were splayed across his chest and he gingerly lifted them away, before he lit a kerosene lamp and left for the outhouse.

The tepid air was sweet with the scent of burning palo santo, and the bushes bristled and chirped with the symphony of crickets. He missed when he and his family had a real bathroom to use, with clean running water, bright lights, and glimmering mirrors, before his father went missing at the Kingston Port a year earlier. Wealth-hungry in-laws swooped in shortly after, throwing Talk-Straight, his toddler siblings, and pregnant mother onto the street. They'd lived in the cemetery ever since.

Arriving at the outhouse, he slammed the rickety wood door shut and began emptying his bladder into the rancid pit.

Soon, Talk-Straight heard footsteps stamping through the dirt, circling the outhouse.

"Hello?" Talk-Straight called. "Somebody there?"

Impatient knocking sounded at the door, and his breath quickened while his heart fell to his ankles.

"Hey! I'm pissing!" he shouted, pretending to seem angry. "Don't rush me!"

The air grew cold and a sly; a smoky cackle echoed

behind his ear. Talk-Straight bolted from the outhouse as though his shoes were filled with hot coals, only to find the lone kerosene lamp burning orange through the dark.

With a trembling hand, he reached down to the lamp's handle.

"Talk-Straight!" a low male voice whispered.

The boy jumped. "Who's there? Show yourself, I'll knock you out!"

"You too rude!" the voice answered, indignant. "You want hurt me when me want help you?"

"W...who are you?"

"I'm Roy." Puffs of tobacco smoke flowed ahead of Talk-Straight, as though the outline of a man was enjoying a pipe.

"M-Mister Roy like the one who they buried today?" Talk-Straight stuttered. "B-b-but you're dead. Are you—"

A deep inhale silenced him. Followed by a deep exhale and trail of smoke.

"You 'fraid a duppy, boy?" the voice bellowed.

Talk-Straight breathed in sharply as chills crept up his spine, smooth and slow like water filling a glass. Like most people on the island, he'd heard of duppies before—been warned of them. It was a term that meant 'ghost' or 'demon' but in actuality, neither of these terms fit nor did they accurately describe what a duppy actually is. While listening to the bedtime stories of his long-departed grandmother, Talk-Straight learned that a duppy could be a fusion of a demon, ghost, and more. Malevolent or benign; a mixture of light, dark, and all in between. They crept along the fringes of the ancestral world and the land of the living, with powers and intentions that few understood. Talk-Straight's grandmother warned that duppies could be *anything*, and since one never knew who or what they were truly dealing with, it was safest to avoid them. This uncertainty twisted like a dagger in his gut and he hid his hands behind his back, hoping the duppy hadn't seen how badly they were shaking.

"All dis time me hear seh you talk straight, no?" the duppy said gently. "So come make we talk straight—aha, let us discuss certain matters. Young man, I would like to go to church."

"Why does a duppy want to go to church?"

"Why don't *you* want to go to church?"

Talk-Straight swallowed hard as his heart thumped and Roy let out a dry cackle.

"No matta. Now, listen carefully—we need to go to the beach tomorrow and collect some sand. Meet me under the poinciana tree near the front gate at 3PM. If you do as I ask, you and your family will never want for anything again."

"Why should I believe you?" Talk-Straight asked, an eyebrow arched.

"Because I'm already helping you."

As the smoke faded into the night air, Talk-Straight felt something hard and cool beneath his tongue. He reached into his mouth, pulling out a pebble-sized chunk of gold.

The next day at 3PM, Talk-Straight went by the blooming poinciana tree, its magenta flowers raining like confetti across the gray tombstones. His mother was busy tending to a boiling pot as his siblings kicked up dirt and chased small lizards. An invisible weight fell onto his shoulders and Talk-Straight nearly dropped to his knees.

"Shh..." a voice hushed in his ear, making the hairs on his neck stand up.

"R-Roy? What are you doing on my back?" Talk-Straight asked.

"Walk. *Now.*"

"I can't, you're too heavy!"

"Talk-Straight, who you a' talk to?" his mother called, "You don't see I need help?!"

"Walk. Now." the voice repeated with a hiss.

"Ah...sorry Mama, I have to go to work now," he said, taking pained steps towards the cemetery exit.

"Work? In the *evening*?" she cried.

"Yeah, at a restaurant washing dishes. I'll be back soon."

Talk-Straight trudged to the beach panting, rank sweat sopped around his armpits, his feet felt heavy as lead, and his head throbbed with pain.

"Roy? Why can't you just walk on your own two feet?" he breathed.

Roy chuckled. "Me eva did tell you me have feet?"

Talk-Straight immediately thought Roy may have had them amputated while he was alive—if he were ever alive in the first place. He kept his imagination from wandering any further.

Arriving at the beach, he collapsed into a stupor on his knees, the indigo ocean fading in and out of focus in his vision, thirst cracking the insides of his throat.

"Fill your pockets with all the sand they can hold," Roy instructed, "Then meet me by the outhouse at midnight with your 'stove' and pot."

"I'm going to look like a madman if I'm alone on the beach, stuffing sand in my pockets!" Talk-Straight cried. "What do you plan to do with it anyway?"

"Something *quite* special," Roy replied. "Now...get to work."

Talk-Straight felt something cold and hard beneath his tongue again and reached into his mouth—another pebble of gold, slightly larger this time. He slipped the rock between his gum and cheek, and began filling his pockets with sand. He grimaced when a trio of teen-aged boys on bicycles stopped to point and laugh at him. His eyes sliced them up and down: they wore crisp clothes and clean shoes that were worth more than he could earn in a month.

"Look at that crazy boy!" one howled. "And his dirty clothes!"

"He must be poor!" another laughed, "And my father told me poor people don't have *no* sense!"

One of the boys snorted. "Denzel, your father is a pastor and he talk dat way 'bout poor people?"

"Of course! Look at his mouth!" Denzel said with a crooked smile, "You t'ink he's eating di sand?"

The third boy jeered. "Dunno! Make we slap it outta him mouth just in case!"

Soon enough, Talk-Straight found himself surrounded by the boys, balling up his fists. They were all much larger than he was. He couldn't speak—not wanting to give the gold away; he couldn't run either—his pockets weren't full of sand yet.

One of the boys flung sand into his eyes and Talk-

Straight kicked him in the shins, while another boy twisted around, punching him in the jaw. The burdensome weight suddenly shifted off his shoulders and Talk-Straight fell straight onto his bottom, a hand over his bleeding mouth. Batting sand from his face, he heard muffled screams and smelled the stench of urine.

Looking around, he saw that all three boys lay twitching and choking in the sand, white eyes in their heads and foam flowing from their mouths. One of them had even soiled himself. Talk-Straight's heart raced as he hurried to complete his task, finding the weight had returned atop him worse than before.

"Such silly boys," the voice said with a deep laugh. "They couldn't even handle a single slap from me! Go home, young man. You've done well."

Talk-Straight plucked the gold from his mouth, slick with blood after biting his tongue.

"Put it in your pocket," the voice commanded. "I want the blood."

"But what about these boys?" Talk-Straight asked, "I can't leave them here. They were nasty and brutish, but I should still find them a doctor."

"Why help those with more than you?" the voice asked, "Let them help themselves."

"Roy...is it you who's making people disappear?" asked Talk-Straight.

He winced inwardly when no response came.

Moments later, the voice answered. "No. You ever see somebody disappear yet?" Its teasing, care-free tone filled the young man's mind and body with a strange coldness.

A car rumbled by and Talk-Straight jumped. He reasoned that it was best he return home before anyone saw him. Talk-Straight punched his hands into his pockets hard enough to ensure neither sand nor gold would escape and trekked home as the sun set.

At midnight, Talk-Straight had set up the stove and pot as Roy had asked.

"You a' do good, my youth!" Roy said, "Now, put the sand to cook."

"Let's use a bucket, I can't put sand in Mama's pot," Talk-Straight said. "She'll slap me! And everything we eat afterwards will have grains of sand in it."

Roy kissed his teeth. "Talk-Straight, I know you're tired but I need you to *think*-straight right now. How many pots do you think you can buy with the gold I gave you?"

Talk-Straight let out a defeated sigh. "Many. Anyway, the sand is looking a little strange, Roy...it has a green and black tint to it. What happened?"

"You'll see."

Talk-Straight started the fire. He'd used a tin can to store the sand earlier, and poured it into the pot, stirring counter-clockwise every time Roy told him to. Soon, its color changed to green and black, glowing like flakes of flame and ash. Moving his wooden spoon about, he thought he'd heard the sound of a boy crying.

"Stir, stir!" Roy encouraged.

As Talk-Straight stirred, the faces of the three boys on the beach appeared, warped and clumpy as porridge. The sand screamed and screamed as Talk-Straight pulled gold kernels from his jaw one after the other. Fear scratched at the back of his mind, so he shifted his thoughts to his mother and siblings that evening; how they only had mangoes to eat for dinner while the boys' bicycles, shoes and clothes were worth enough to feed them for months. How the boys laughed and jeered at him, how they rode and wore money without a care in the world.

Suddenly, the sound of each nugget clunking into the tin can filled him with satisfaction as Talk-Straight banged his wooden spoon hard against the edge of the pot, the faces in the sand stretching like gum and wailing.

"Now what?" he asked.

"Now, we're ready to go to church," Roy replied.

The next day, Talk-Straight stood underneath the blooming poinciana tree in his Sunday best: a navy blue suit he hadn't worn in over a year. It was a bit too tight around his hips and definitely too short at his ankles, but Roy had assured him they were simply going to throw tithes and listen to a hymn or two.

In his hands was the tin of sand and a heaviness fell on his shoulders again, bringing him to his knees.

"Whoa! Don't break my back!" he griped, getting back up. "I had to throw out Mama's pot yesterday. Let's get to the church before she finds out 'cause she'll beat me for sure then."

"Leave the sand in the pastor's office," the voice on his shoulders said, its breath hot and moist against his cheek.

Talk-Straight dragged his feet to church, the weight of

the duppy on his shoulders causing him to nearly collapse twice during the short walk.

Approaching the church gates, he noticed a sparkling white car parked by the curb. As people entered, some of the parishioners looked Talk-Straight up and down with trepidation. Some gave warm greetings while others had smiles so fake, they may as well have had been nailed to their faces. An old woman in a pink dress and hat hobbled up to the gates with her cane.

"Are you here to wash the pastor's car?" she asked innocently, "One should never work on the Sabbath, you know."

Talk-Straight shook his head. "No, Madame. He said he'll do it himself."

Once inside, Talk-Straight took a seat near the back of the church as an organ began to play, the music slow and melancholic. The congregation stood and started singing while Talk-Straight mouthed nonsense to appear as if he knew the words. A solemn Pastor Boyce approached the pulpit next, followed by a middle-aged woman dressed entirely in black. Frowning, she dabbed a handkerchief at her eyes and the mascara running down her cheeks. After everyone had sat down, pastor Boyce began to speak.

"Thank you Lord for giving us this day," he said. "As some of you may know, we lost our son Denzel recently." He took a breath. "He was only sixteen years old. We would've loved to have him longer, watch him grow into a gentleman. But the Lord giveth and taketh for reasons that we, as mortals, may never understand. Funeral arrangements will be announced shortly and I thank you all for your condolences and support."

Numb, Talk-Straight slouched in his seat, the humidity crushing him as the room spun in a mess of colors and hats. The jar of sand next to him seemed to screech long and loud as a kettle and Talk-Straight put his head between his knees to avoid throwing up.

Talk-Straight jolted awake to an empty church. *How long had he slept?*

Looking out the window, he saw that the sun had already begun to set, fresh panic coursing through his veins.

Did Mama find out about the pot? Did his siblings have something to eat? When should he tell Mama about the gold and would she believe him? Maybe she didn't need to know...

"Sand! Office!" the voice barked in his ear; Talk-Straight wincing.

He peered around and seeing no one, crept towards the pastor's office. Twisting the knob, he found that the door was locked. Talk-Straight let out an aggravated sigh until he heard several clicks on the other side—the door gently creaked open.

He took a deep breath, expecting to see a fire-and-brimstone-faced pastor, but was met with a spacious room with a large window and cherry oak desk with a Bible. Rushing in, he quickly placed the tin of sand on the desk but before he could run back out, the door slammed in his face.

"I've unlocked the closet for you too, young man,"

Roy said. "Take a *good* look."

Cautiously, Talk-Straight pulled the closet door open. Inside, on the middle shelf, were a large jagged dagger and a statue of an angel with bat-like wings. It had sat upon some money and was adorned with jewellery. Etched at his feet, were the words: *All these things I will give You if You will fall down and worship me. Matthew 4:9.*

Something knocked against his foot and Talk-Straight looked down to see a toddler-size shoe. He crouched down, finding a pile of clothes: small and large trousers and dresses, ties and necklaces, along with several other pairs of shoes encrusted with crimson. One tie, in particular, caught his eye, so he reached in and took it. It was navy blue and had the initials "HBS" knitted into its tip in bright yellow. Only one person he knew had such embroidery done on their ties: his father, Horace Brown Senior.

"Daddy?" he whimpered to himself, holding the tie tenderly. Tears swelled in his eyes as he put it in his pocket.

"Hey! What are you doing in my office?!"

Talk-Straight jumped up and turned to see Pastor Boyce glaring at him. "I'm talking to you! Come here!" he roared, snatching Talk-Straight by his shirt collar. "Who told *you* to open *my* door and go through *my* things?!"

"Let *me* go!" Talk-Straight yelled. "Murderer!"

"Shut your mouth!"

Pastor Boyce growled and wrapped his thick hands around Talk-Straight's neck, squeezing so hard the veins in his neck and forehead throbbed through his skin. "You stinking thief!" he seethed, "I'll throw another tithe for riches tonight boy, and it's you!"

Talk-Straight grabbed onto Boyce's wrists struggling to free himself, but his skinny arms were no match for the large man, and his lungs burned for air.

The lights in the church cut out.

The ground beneath their feet quaked angrily before coming to an abrupt stop, and a cold wind that reeked of rotting meat filled the room as whispers echoed from the walls and ceiling.

Boyce loosened his grip and Talk-Straight inhaled with a gasp. Pastor Boyce gagged and placed a hand over his nose and mouth, while the other clung to Talk-Straight's shirt collar. He watched as the tin of sand on the desk turned such a blazing red that a circle of flames jutted out from beneath it, and Boyce's eyes grew wide as the church's doors when he screamed.

"Lord Jesus, have mercy!" he cried. "No demon shall prosper here!"

"Not. Even. You!" the voices thundered from the walls.

Talk-Straight stomped on Boyce's foot and tussled himself free, bolting out of the room. He sprinted through the church doors and down the street, Boyce's terrified shrieks mingling with smoky cackles from behind him.

Arriving home at sunset, Talk-Straight's mother hugged and kissed him.

"Me son! Me son!" she cried, squeezing him with one arm, the cooing infant in the other. "Is like one miracle! Imagine, I was searchin' for di pot dis mornin' and found it full o'gold!" she laughed. "You alright? You look sad."

Talk-Straight nodded. "I'm fine, Mommy. Just coming from Church, tired."

"Oh! And what did the pastor talk about today?"

The weary young boy stood dazed for a moment, his mind numbed by fatigue and fear.

"...Money," he answered, "How people will do anything for money."

Talk-Straight watched his baby sister nibbling her fist, smiling at him.

"Daisy's better now," his mother said with a beaming grin. "Don't worry, son. We are going to do great things with our money. Come! Make we catch one taxi and go a' one hotel. Tomorrow, me a' go buy we one big house! And now I can afford you school fee! Boy...wish you daddy coulda see dis!"

Talk-Straight held his mother tightly, swallowing the tears ready to break.

"Me too, Mama. I'll meet you at the gate. I have to go to the bathroom *very* badly."

"All right. Don't take too long."

Talk-Straight strode over to the outhouse where he first vomited before relieving himself—but at least his shoulders felt light as ever.

Outside, he heard a skidding, shuffling noise moving across the dry earth, as though someone was kicking a soccer ball.

"Roy?" he called.

"Good work, my youth," the voice answered, "Now—go meet your mother at the gate. You don't want duppy to 'ketch you a' night fall."

Talk-Straight laughed. "But you are a duppy, Roy."

He left the outhouse to see splotches of blood on the ground. Five giant, inverted handprints stomped across the dirt in a walking motion, before disappearing behind a nest of bushes.

A deep cackle. "Roy? What is *dat*? Who Roy? Which Roy you talkin'? Do you really know what, who, which duppy you *really* been dealin' with?"

A rustle echoed from the bushes and Talk-Straight's heart galloped with fear. Who or what had he been talking to all this time? What was the duppy—a ghost, demon, monster, all of the above, or something in between? How many were there? The chills he'd felt listening to his grandmother's bedtime duppy stories and warnings returned and grew tenfold, raking down his back as biting his toes he realized his folly. He had no clue who or what he was dealing with.

"You tink Roy is di only duppy out here?" the phantom continued, "Oh, what sweet wickedness we did get to eat this day! Don't have *no reason* to hang 'round you and your family hut no more..."

The duppy burst into an indiscernible language mixed with Patois curse words. Shadowy claws rose Pastor Boyce's bloody head from behind the bush, its bloated face filled with gravel and mouth twisted into an eternal scream.

"'Cause we done get what we want!"

A gust of frigid air blasted into Talk Straight's face as a blanket of sand rose over his head, covering his body and stinging like the devil. The boy screamed and sprinted from the cemetery, while the duppy's laughter transformed from a cackle into a chorus of hysterical howls he would never forget.

Ainsley Hawthorn

Ainsley Hawthorn, Ph.D., is a cultural historian, author, and multidisciplinary artist. Raised in Steady Brook, Newfoundland & Labrador, and now based in St. John's, she earned her doctorate in Near Eastern Languages and Civilizations at Yale University.

Hawthorn is passionate about using her academic knowledge to bring new ideas about culture, history, and religion to a general audience.

As a public scholar, she blogs for *Psychology Today*, writes for CBC, and has contributed to various other publications, including *The Globe and Mail*, the *National Post*, and the *Newfoundland Quarterly*.

She edited the anthology *Land of Many Shores: Stories from a Diverse Newfoundland and Labrador*, and is currently completing her first solo-authored non-fiction book, *The Other Five Senses*.

Previous From the Rock series credits include 'The Patchwork Skin' in *Mythology from the Rock*.

She brings with her her story, 'Every Child a Changeling.'

Every Child a Changeling

"To the English the witches, to the Irish the fairies."

That's what Mother used to say like a moral when she finished a story of glamours or enchantments, May trees, or underground mansions. She murmured it like an admonishment, too, if we fidgeted as she slipped breadcrumbs from our breakfast plates into our pockets before we ran off to play in the meadows above the cove.

She said it less and less, though, after Bridget was born.

I never considered Mother a superstitious woman. The day Father started coughing up blood, she went out into the garden and spent the afternoon calmly dyeing all but one of her dresses black. I often wonder if Father could see them from the window as he lay in bed, fluttering darkly in the wind like mourning drapes while he choked on the air that blew by them.

With five little ones to raise after he was gone, Mother couldn't abide nonsense and would scold us for taletelling if we spoke of playing at pirates or being afeared of boo-darbies in the root cellar. Between milking the goats and weeding the garden, scrubbing laundry for the merchants, and darning our socks to last another season, her hours were too full for fantasy.

No, she wasn't superstitious, only practical. She threw dishwater over the embers at night to prevent fire, stored hay in the cockloft to prevent rot, and put crumbs in our pockets to prevent devilry. The good people, the gentle folk, weren't a legend then. They were our neighbours, and we lived alongside them in familiar if uneasy relation.

Two baby boys born after me and before Bridget hadn't survived. James died in the womb and was born still, though the priest told Mother he lived long enough to be baptized. My eldest sister, Myrtle, remembered seeing him swaddled up in his miniature casket on the dining room table. She told me he looked like a shriveled old man.

Mother dozed off nursing Joseph and woke to find him blue at her breast. For all she slapped his round cheeks and rubbed his barrel chest, she could not wake him, and she could never be convinced afterward that she hadn't smothered him in her sleep.

They laid Father to rest alongside his sons' little graves where the turf was already sagging into the ground like a worn-out mattress, and Mother had all three of their names carved together on a marble headstone with space left over for her own.

Bridget was born within the year with fair, downy hair, and iris-blue eyes. We all of us in our family had the Celtic aspect – blond hair that favoured the strawberry and pale, freckled skin that burnt in the sun – and Bridget was stamped in our image. She was a boisterous baby who laughed easily and wailed loudly. We sang to her to make her coo and bounced her on our knees to make her giggle.

One evening, Mother was walking home from our auntie's house up the lane with Bridget in one arm and a basket of bread slung over the other when she was surrounded by a flock of horses. There was no small number of ponies around the cove for ploughing and hauling, but these animals were tall and slender, true Arabians like in a storybook. They were all shades of grey – steel, dapple, and rose – and they roamed freely without harness or bridle, watching Mother sidelong with their wide, dark eyes.

She made to edge between two of them blocking her way, but the horses turned about on her then. Pawing at the ground on all sides of her, they pulled back their lips and snapped at the baby with their spade teeth. It's hard to appreciate, if you haven't spent as much time around livestock as we did in small towns in those days, just how big horses are, and how dangerous. With just one kick, even a pony can snap your ribs or crack your skull. A stallion in the harbour over from us was spooked by a boy spinning a wooden noisemaker. The horse reared back and came down on the child's leg. He never walked right again after that.

Mother wrapped her arms around the baby, tucked her head, and ran, keeping one shoulder before her to push past the broad, heavy horse bodies. She burst through the circle of animals, twisting her knee as they parted and tumbled her forward into the dirt, then dashed up the open road to our house. They did not follow, and she did not look back.

In the days afterward, the blue leached out of Bridget's eyes, dimming them to a brown so deep they looked nearly black. Slowly, almost imperceptibly, her pale, feathery hair fell from her head, and in its place grew thick, umber curls. Though we sang to her, she no longer cooed, and, when we bounced her on our knees, she no longer giggled. She sat by the window alone, puppeting twigs and stones as though they were dolls.

"If only I had given some bread to the horses," I heard Mother sigh to herself one day while wringing out the washing, and I asked her what she meant.

"I realized after that all they wanted was a taste of bread. Had I given them one, they would surely have let me pass."

Bridget grew into a pretty, slight young girl. Most days, she would leave the house by herself in the morning and return at dusk with leaves tangled up in her coily hair. Mother would sit her down by the stove and brush them out one by one. Though she would shake her head, Mother never spoke a harsh word to Bridget nor did she ever tell her to stop her solitary ramblings, even when there were whispers in the church that the child was odd.

Now and again Bridget would follow after me through the cove when I went to meet my friends, almost like any ordinary tagalong of a little sister. While we played duck-on-the-rock or cobby houses, she would entertain herself close by, weaving daisy chains or humming to herself while she twirled in circles, around and around. She never joined in with us, and soon the other children stopped asking her to. Invitations gave way to cajoling, teasing, and, eventually, friendly resignation. My friends would incline their heads at her before running off to our games.

I might have been embarrassed at first, but I learned acceptance, too. That's just the way she was, and you can no more fight a child's nature than you can catch the wind. For all her aloofness, Bridget seemed to enjoy the company, the nearness of our bodies and the sound of our voices. She never strayed too far but stayed where she could see and hear us, within the comforting circle of our presence.

She was with me one afternoon when I was playing with the Crockers' girl, Helen. The Crockers were the only Protestant family in the cove, most of them living on the opposite side of the bay in Padstow. For all Uncle Phonse muttered about "those Orange bastards" poaching on his fishing grounds when he thought none of us children could hear him, I couldn't see very much difference between Helen and me, though she did prove Mother right about the witches.

I had never heard tell of a witch until Helen confided that once, when their goats had been giving sour milk, her mother had peed in a jar, stopped it, then laid it up alongside the stove as a charm to expose the witch that had surely cursed them. Miss Renouf down the way had taken sick not long after, the goats' milk had freshened, and Mrs. Crocker had poured her water out in the yard. It all seemed awfully silly to me, but Helen believed in it utterly.

That day, Helen and I were at alleys when we heard a racket at the Lynches' next door. When the two of us hopped the fence between the little houses and crept up to the kitchen window, we saw a group of men gathered around the table – some sitting, some standing – speaking earnestly to one another. Mrs. Lynch was leant back against the counter crying, and Mr. Lynch banged his fist on the table.

Their son, Jake, had gone out to cut wood the previous afternoon and had never come home. The next morning, Jake's horse was at the door, his dray was at the door, but he was nowhere to be found. Jake was a young man of eighteen or twenty years. He still lived with his parents but had a sweetheart in Florence Sullivan, and they were expected to be engaged any time.

Like most men of the cove, Jake was no stranger to the woods. He spent days there chopping, trapping, and shooting. Though not far advanced in years, he should have known the trails and the landmarks well enough to find his way home even if he got turned around. Some of the crowd gathered in the kitchen were reassuring the Lynches that Jake would be back yet, that perhaps he'd gone farther in than he planned, gotten caught by nightfall, and had waited for daylight to make his way out. Mr. Lynch wouldn't hear it. Jake could be injured, he said, and they needed to search for him before the sun went down on another day.

The men began mustering themselves to go out into the forest, and Helen and I crouched down below the window, backs to the white clapboard. It was then that we noticed Bridget was with us, standing riveted a few feet behind, hands hanging at her sides, brow furrowed.

"They won't find Jake Lynch in those woods," she said. "Not today and not tomorrow."

They didn't, either. At nightfall, the men returned empty-handed. All that night and all the next day, rain fell in buckets. No searchers went out, and, from the top of the stairs at home on the second evening, we overheard Uncle Phonse down in the kitchen saying to Mother and Aunt Mildred there was little hope at this rate he'd be found alive.

Bridget was stood up beside my brother Francis as we all of us strained to make out their hushed conversation, and, on hearing this, she rushed down the steps so suddenly that none of us had time to catch the hem of her nightdress to pull her back. She came up short in the kitchen doorway, and, though we couldn't see past the doorframe from our roost on the second floor, the adults must have noticed her, because their conversation soon trailed off.

"Jake Lynch isn't in those woods, Mother. They'll find him tomorrow down by the shore between here and Padstow."

There was a long silence. Thinking back on it, I wonder if it was the first time Auntie Mildred and Uncle Phonse had ever heard Bridget speak. Finally, Mother's voice cut through the close air.

"What makes you say that, child?"

"I just know it," answered Bridget. "Don't ask me how I know it, Mother. I just do."

After a pause, we heard Mother's chair scrape back from the table.

"All right, my love. Come on, then."

She appeared at the door, took Bridget by the shoulder, and, finding the rest of her children crouched guiltily at the top of the stairs, shooed the lot of us back to bed.

Overnight the rain let up, and the next day the search resumed. It wasn't noon yet when Peter Dwyer came upon Jake walking up the landwash from Padstow. Despite being all those days out in the rain, he was dry as a bone from top to toe. Back at the Lynches', wrapped in a blanket before the stove, Jake told the neighbours he couldn't remember a jot about his time away, only going into the woods to haul lumber and, next thing he knew, coming to himself on the shoreline as though no time had passed at all. Uncle Phonse reported it back to us just as he had heard it himself.

The searchers toasted their efforts, and the Lynches were over the moon, as you might well imagine. Jake came to mass that Sunday, clean and neat, and, though his demeanour was sombre, Florence Sullivan sat smiling up at him, holding his hand. At the recessional, they walked out together. Bridget never breathed a word of it again, at least not to me. She went back to her wandering and her dancing, as quiet and distant as ever. Only I was troubled. I kept my thoughts to myself until, some time later, I found myself alone in the garden with Mother, weeding the vegetables.

"Mother," I said, "there's something uncanny about Bridget."

She tutted at me, pushing herself upright then wiping her hands on her apron. She always sat sidelong to work the garden because of her bad knee.

"Now, that foolishness—" she began, but I rushed on. I didn't want to stop talking for fear I'd never be brave enough to say the words again.

"She was a good baby until you met those horses, and everything changed. She's strange. She won't play with us, she hardly speaks, and then, when she does speak, it's about Jake Lynch! How could she have known where they'd find Jake Lynch when he'd been led astray, except by the fairy sight? He was taken by the fairies and our Bridget was taken by the fairies and this Bridget is nothing but a fairy machine, a changeling!"

I was breathless and Mother speechless. Then, she patted the earth beside her with a palm that was calloused but gentle, and, as I scooted closer, she spoke.

"Have you heard of a girl named Ruth Puddester?"

I shook my head.

"No, I didn't expect so. She's a handsome little thing who lives in Padstow. Comes into the cove now and again to collect the mail for her father, since the coastal boat doesn't stop over there. I hear her father's not well and that all he wants is for her to marry a good Anglican man before he dies. She's his only daughter. She must love her father very much."

Mother smoothed her skirt and smiled to herself. I was confused.

"There are many reasons a man might go missing, and many ways that a person might live. You see, love, all children are changelings. They're a bit like the parents who bear them and a bit like the parents who raise them and entirely like their own little selves. They're changed not just once, but many times over, and they're hardly ours for a moment before they go out and make little changelings of their own. Do you understand now?"

"Yes," I said, though I didn't.

It seems like only a short time after that day, in the way childhood passes in a kind of reverie, that I met a nice Catholic boy who worked the coastal boats. We married, and I went out West with him to Stephenville, where we sowed our own garden and started our own family. My brothers and sisters did the same, scattering to the four winds like dandelion seeds. All, that is, except Bridget, who stayed in our home in the cove to the day Mother's name was engraved in marble beside her husband's and sons' and Bridget inherited the house.

It wasn't until many years later, until I had a daughter of my own, perfect and strange, a bit like me and entirely like herself, until I brought my daughter to visit shy Auntie Bridget who took her on long nature walks, the two of them laughing together at things only they could hear, that I came to know what my mother meant. I'll place no bread in my daughter's pockets. Instead, I'll lay up my expectations alongside the stove and let her live among the fairies.

ON THE COVER

The cover image to this year's anthology was was created by Graham Blair of Graham Blair Designs.

Graham Blair is an artist and designer living in St. John's, Newfoundland. His time is split between graphic design (www.grahamblairdesigns.com) and making traditional-method woodcut prints (www.grahamblairwoodcuts.com).

Much of his work incorporates folkloric themes and nods to regional traditions.

FAIRY TALES
FROM THE ROCK
EDITED BY ERIN VANCE AND ELLEN CURTIS

In the beginning, fairy tales were all we had.

Tales to explain the unexplained, to impart morality, and culture. But more often than not, to warn.

From the editors of the From the Rock anthologies comes a new selection of stories, carefully curated from some of Newfoundland and Labrador's favourite authors. Between these pages, old tales are revisited, familiar foes lurk, and fairy tales for the modern age are born.

Including the work of Bronwynn Erskine (*By Reservation Only*), Melissa Bishop (*The Fairies of Foggy Island*) and David James Lynch (*All Things Broken*).

Manufactured by Amazon.ca
Bolton, ON